THE OTHER SIDE OF DA COURT

by
T.R. REED

PublishAmerica

Baltimore

First printing

ISBN: 1-4137-1383-1
PUBLISHED BY PUBLISHAMERICA, LLLP
www.publishamerica.com
Baltimore

Printed in the United States of America

To my Lord, my strength and my light. Thank you for the continued gift of life and the blessing of this talent. I pray that I might touch someone's life as you have touched mine.

To my mother, Virgie, for your wisdom, guidance and spiritual growth. Thank you for instilling a good heart and determination in me. I will carry your loving spirit with me always.

To my father, James, for your wisdom, guidance and friendship. Thank you for always listening and making me laugh when I really wanted to cry. Your support has been a rock in my life.

To my sister, Valerie, for your unconditional sisterly love. No other sister-friend could ever love and understand me more.

To Jermaine, my love, my hope, my friend, my future. Thank you for calming me and bringing me peace when I had no cause for peace. Thank you for the continuous support on my good and bad days. This is for us.

6/27/04

Gwen,

Thank you for the love,
encouragement and support.

Love Always,

Tanya

PROLOGUE

August 1982

"Down, down baby...down by the roller coaster...sweet, sweet baby...I'll never let you go..."

"Lisa," her mother calls.

"Yes?"

"Are you jumping rope in the house again?"

"No."

"I think you are. How many times do I have to tell you, jumping rope is for outdoors."

"But..."

"But nothing. Please do not jump rope in the house. Now, are you ready to go?"

Eight-year-old Lisa bolts from her bedroom and runs down the hall. She greets her mother in the living room of their Bronx apartment. Her mother is turning the fan's speed down to low, so the house can remain cool while they are out. She makes swift movements around the room, turning off the television and locking the side windows. As she turns around to call Lisa again, she almost topples over her. Lisa's three-foot frame stands at her feet, smiling like sunshine.

"Sweetie, you startled me," she says, looking down at her little gem.

"I'm sorry, Mommy. I'm ready to go."

"Let me look at you."

Mrs. Nichols places her hands on her slender hips and gives her daughter a quick once over. A few strands of blonde hair have parted their way from the ponytails she had made this morning. Lisa's yellow and white floral sundress is a tad wrinkled but in acceptable condition. Mrs. Nichols gently pulls her own dress up slightly, and kneels down to Lisa's height. She brushes her baby girl's hair back into place and smooths out her dress. That's when she notices the sneakers.

"Lisa, why do you have sneakers on with your dress? Where are your sandals?"

"Mommy, I don't want to wear my sandals. They hurt my feet and I can't jump rope in them."

"Young lady, go put on your sandals, please. We're not going outside for you to play. We're going to have dinner in a nice restaurant."

"I don't want to wear them. Melinda doesn't have to wear sandals." She frowns.

"Go," her mother emphasizes her statement with a tap on Lisa's behind.

Lisa runs down the hall and back into her room. The jump rope she still held tightly gets thrown on the bed. She opens her closet and reaches towards the back, near the wall. She had placed the brand new box all the way in the corner, so she could say she lost them later. Lisa sits on the bed and kicks off her white canvas sneakers. She exchanges them for white straps and buckles.

"You're moving in slow motion, pumpkin," her mother calls.

Lisa tries to hurry but she isn't excited about wearing the constraining wedge heels, or going out to dinner. She wanted to play jump rope with Melinda in front of the building. But she does as she is told and puts on her shoes.

Slowly, she clogs her way back down the hall, where her mother stands at the front door, keys in hand.

"Now, that's better. Let's go. We're going to be late picking up Daddy."

"Daddy's coming too?" Her frown flips upside down. She beams at the thought of her daddy joining them for a night out. She wonders where they are going to eat, and if Daddy will let her get a sundae for dessert. She knows Mommy won't like it, but Daddy would say yes. He always knows how to give her what she wants, without Mommy protesting.

The two hurry from the fifth floor and onto the elevator. Lisa likes to watch the buttons light up whenever someone pushes them. She wants to see what will happen once they were all lit. Will the elevator go crazy? Will it take them to every floor and back again? She is tempted to push them, but she knows that's a no-no. Today, the stainless steel interior looks like new. It's polished to perfection and the two admire themselves in the mirror images before them. On the first floor, they bump into the lady that smells funny, as Lisa thinks. She gives Mrs. Johnson her pretty smile like her mother had taught her, and they walk out of the building and down the street.

Lisa tries to remain excited about going to dinner with Daddy. But it is difficult because the kids across the street are out playing. Lisa wants to dart over and play hop-scotch with them. The kids in the brownstones always have fun games to play. She joins them only when her mother sits on the stoop of their building to watch. Her excitement fades as one of them calls out to her, asking her to come play. She gives her friend a look that reads "I can't, maybe tomorrow" and lets her mother lead her down the street, past all of the fun.

They walk to the end of their block and cross the street. Mrs. Nichols tells her daughter to walk a little faster, stop lagging behind, gaping at the boys playing basketball in the court. Lisa is mesmerized by all the boys who are out playing today. She recognizes a few from her class but doesn't dare call out to them. Her mother would be mad if she knew that occasionally she and Mel sneak down to the court and talk to the boys.

"Lisa, come on, we're going to be late getting your father."

"Okkkaaaayyyyy," she whines.

"Aren't you excited about going to Daddy's school? 'Mr. Bones' is still there and you know how much you love him," Mrs. Nichols tries to convince her.

Lisa perks up at the sound of that. Her mother is right, she does love "Mr. Bones," the skeleton that stands in the back of her father's classroom. He uses it to teach his students basic anatomy and science. Every time she visits her daddy at school, he shows her a new body part and tells her what it does. She is fascinated by it. Then all the way home, she would recite the name and try to remember what that organ does. Last time, he explained what the main artery of the heart does. But she couldn't remember the name of it. She decides to ask her father again when she gets there.

Mrs. Nichols and Lisa continue past the basketball court and further down the street. The tree-lined streets they walk end at the edge of the park. They jay-walk through a busy intersection and leave the residential area behind them. The city is filled with skyscrapers and swarms of people. Lisa and her mother dart in and out of traffic because people and cars are everywhere. The two pass delis and shops along the way.

They stop briefly in front of the boutique that Mrs. Nichols likes to shop in. Lisa watches her mother eye a few dresses and a grey pants suit through the store window.

"Are we going in today, Mommy? You would look pretty in that pants suit."

"No, not today, pumpkin. We'll come back another time. I'm sure it will still be here next week."

"Are you sure? I know Daddy will love you in it," Lisa presses. She liked to shop with her mother and watch her try on clothes. Mrs. Nichols is the prettiest mother in the world, Lisa thinks.

"No, I won't go in today. Maybe tomorrow. C'mon."

Just a few more blocks and they approach the store-front office where Lisa's father works. The outside window has blue lettering sprayed on it, inviting anyone in who wants to read, write or obtain their diploma. Originally a one-room school that rented the back of the building, the establishment now flourished as owners of the entire office space. There were five classrooms in the back, one office and even a receptionist's desk when you walk in the door. That's where Lisa and her mother stand, waiting for Annette to greet them.

"Hmm, that's odd. Annette is not at her desk. C'mon, we'll check the office," Mrs. Nichols says.

A few steps down the hall and they reach the office. All of the teachers, including Lisa's father, share the office. It is a mess! Papers, books, chalk boxes, everything is thrown all over the place.

"No one's in there either. I wonder where your father is."

Then voices come from further down the hall. They seem to come from one of the classrooms. Lisa follows her mother down the long hallway, just as curious. She also wonders why Annette isn't sitting at her desk, she is always there. But then she remembers "Mr. Bones" and her question for her father. She is anxious to get to the classroom and find her father. Bounding down the hall, the voices grow louder and sound high pitched. The nearer to the voices they get, the more worried Lisa's mother looks.

Finally, the two stand outside of the last classroom. The door is slightly ajar and the people inside are talking very loud.

"Patrick?" Mrs. Nichols calls as she pushes the door open for her and Lisa to walk inside.

Lisa looks around the room at the grown-ups who are yelling at each other. There is Lorretta, her mother's best friend; Daddy; "Mr. Giant," who lives in her building. And the rest of the people she doesn't know. She watches the adults argue and shakes her head. They are always arguing about something. She had eavesdropped many times and heard them talking about not being able to pay the bills for the school. But somehow the arguing always ended with a quiet solution suggested by her father.

Not phased by the scene, Lisa catches the eye of "Mr. Bones" in the back of the classroom. Without noticing, her mother had grabbed her hand to keep her close. Lisa squirms to free herself from the clutches of her mother. She finally breaks free and runs in front of the adults, down the aisle of desks, and stops in front of "Mr. Bones." She finds the heart and tries to ask her father what the artery's name is.

"Daddy, what's the name of this artery again?" But her voice won't carry over all of the bickering.

She stands marveling at the skeleton. The grown–ups' fight is escalating. She thinks to herself, "How come they get to yell when I can't?" She tries to ask her father again, but he still doesn't hear her. This time she yells her question in desperation.

BUCK!

Lisa covers her ears at the piercing noise that comes from the front of the classroom. "What is that?" she thinks. The ringing in her inner ear tells her to keep her hands over them, until it stops. The bickering stops too. She turns around to see what is the source of that noise, perhaps a new teaching tool Daddy had bought. Whatever it is, she doesn't like it.

"Why are all the grown-ups crying?" she thinks to herself.

"Daddy, I asked you a question." Lisa walks towards the front of the classroom.

"Daddy?"

"Daddy!"

CHAPTER ONE

June, 1989

"So what are you going to do with your summer?" I recall my guidance counselor Ms. Reynolds asking on the last day of school.

"Nothing."

"What do you mean nothing?"

"I mean, I'm going to do absolutely nothing. I'm going to hang with my friends and chill out. Maybe go to a few parties, you know, things like that."

"Lisa, why don't you do something constructive this summer?"

"Tsk." I sucked my teeth at her.

"Seriously. Why don't you read a few books, visit a museum, take a pre-college course."

"Ms. Reynolds, no offense, but please. I don't intend to do any learning this summer."

"Don't you think it would be beneficial if you did? Your grades are excellent and it's time you've thought about your future."

"I don't think so."

"Lisa, all year I've asked you about your plans for the future. Most kids your age already know what they want to do, what they want to achieve. And every time I ask, you avoid the question. What's the problem?"

"I don't have a problem. It's just not something I think about."

"Why? Does this have to do with your father?"

I stand in silence, backing away from her desk.

"Lisa, are you using your past as an excuse not to think about a

promising future? You have to overcome whatever you're feeling.
You have to choose to move on."
   "I don't have to do anything but live."

* * *

WHAT?! You ain't never seen a white girl on the stoop of a
project, right in the heart of the blackest neighborhood in the
Bronx?? I'm 'bout to get vexed. But then my ace boon Melinda
whispers, "Lisa, she just said excuse me, let the girl by." So I slide
over so this bourgeois sister can walk up the steps. She looks mad hot
and mad corny in that prissy yellow sundress and grocery store
sneakers. I should trip her. Mel must have read my mind 'cause she
drops me a look that says, "Trip her and let's gank her for whatever's
in that box of hers." But I chill. For two reasons. One, it's too damn
hot. And two, there'll be plenty of time to teach the new meat about
this hood. She'll get to see all too quickly who's running things up in
here. She'll get to know me, Lisa Nichols.

Le-Le, as my crew calls me affectionately. Yeah, I'm as white as
they come. Yeah, I live in the ghetto. And yeah, this here is my turf.
Don't nobody fuck with me and mine. Some people say I've got a
chip on my shoulder. They think I'm mad because I wasn't born
black; because I act black. I don't know what they're talking about.
What's this "acting" shit! I'm not acting; I'm just me. Black folks is
all I know. I was born in this neighborhood and I'll probably die in
this neighborhood. My skin may be white, but my blood is just as red
as all of my people's blood. We are one in the same. So that "acting
black" shit doesn't even phase me. I'm just me. A product of the
environment my Daddy placed me in.

See, back in the 60s, New York—shit, the country—was all up in
turmoil. I mean America was a mess. Let me fill you in if you didn't
know. The country talked of war with Cuba, over something about an
ocean of pigs. Blacks brawled with whites over the right to sit in the
same room; and women spat at men 'cause they wanted to be treated
as equals. Well, in the midst of all that nonsense, there stood my

father, Mr. Patrick J. Nichols. Pops thought he could make a difference in all of that chaos. So as soon as he shook the hand of his Ivy League dean, took his Ivy League teacher's diploma, and confiscated his trust money, Pops left New Haven, Connecticut, and took the Merritt Parkway south. Never to return to the uppity hills of Connecticut. Well maybe for an occasional holiday, but that's it. Mr. Nichols found a prime location right in the heart of the Bronx where he would open a learning center. His dream: to teach and educate the black man; to help them stand on their own, in the midst of an unequal society. Yep, Pops was a radical for change. Mad people still respect him for that.

Too bad he ain't around to see the fruit of his labor. Too bad he ain't around to see the men, women, and children he taught. Who've left the neighborhood to make more money than he ever made. Too bad he ain't around because he was too naive not to watch his back. Too naive to ever believe that one of the pour souls he helped would turn on him like flies on shit. Too bad he never survived that shot to the neck. See, he died when I was eight. From what I hear, he wouldn't give some low life his GED and the man turned a gun on Pops. Pops tried to talk his way out but the brother shot him just the same.

Yo, mad love to my pops for wanting to do something positive. Mad respect for giving me life. But yo, I ain't going out like that. I may only be 15, but I'm smart enough to know, trust nobody. I've seen too much shit go down right here on this stoop to be trusting anybody. Believe me. My moms, my family, even my girl Melinda; I keep everyone at arm's length. Just far enough away to blade 'em and run.

* * *

The mid-June New York sun beat down on the city like a bully on his after-school victim. Channel 2 meteorologist Mr. G. forecasted that the summer of 1989 would be the hottest in about a decade. He wasn't lying. It is 9:30 and it is already 90! Melinda had called me at

6:30, our normal time to get up for school, and I yelled at her, "Girl, school's out!" And on top of that, it's Saturday!

"Damn, Le," she had said. "You know my body's still on the same schedule. It's only been two days since school let out."

"Don't worry about it," I told her. "I was up anyway."

"Yo, it is hot! And it's supposed to get hotter."

She had suggested we chill today. She only suggested that 'cause the last two days we were out running the streets, hooking up with friends from school. She got in trouble for coming in at 1 a.m. this morning and her mom put her on punishment. Melinda's mom is cool. She watches everything Mel does. Ms. Green doesn't play when it comes to Mel's behavior. I guess she used to beat Mel really bad until a neighbor called the cops on her. The pigs caught her about to rip Mel's hide up with a frying pan. Then Ms. Green chilled. But she still keeps a watchful eye and a hard hand in the assumed position, just in case. That's why I think Mel is like that sometimes. She's always testing the waters. Seeing what she can get away with next. And when she gets caught, I guess those flashbacks come on strong and she chills for a few days.

Mel's lucky though. At least her mom lays down the law. My mom works at night and usually has no idea what I'm doing. During the day she sleeps, in preparation for her 2nd shift night job as a nurse at Mount Vernon Hospital. The only thing my mom hawks me about are my grades. That's all I hear, "Get good grades, so you can get us out of here." Here, meaning the ghetto. Mom's been tripping about leaving the Bronx ever since Pops passed. "These people will kill us and not think twice." "Intelligence and money is all it takes to set ourselves free." Blah, blah, blah. That's all I hear. She wants to leave, I want to stay. She wants me to go to college, I could care less.

Anyway, Mel had suggested we chill out on this stoop. But it was Saturday, and I had planned to grocery shop first. Seems like I do everything around my house. But shopping didn't take long. Thank goodness the Food Lion is only three blocks down. I don't know why some folks around here take the bus or the train all the way into Manhattan to food shop. It's ridiculous when there's a store around the way. Then they complain, their Saturdays are never long enough to get everything done. That's cause their stupid asses are waiting on the Beeline or Metro North all damn day. I don't see anything wrong with the Food Lion's food. I've been grocery shopping since I was old enough to cross the street. Cooking since before that! And not once have I gotten rotten eggs or bad meat. I think these people just want a quick getaway from the norm, so they head into busier, more expensive Manhattan.

Earlier, when I had knocked on Mel's door, she opened the door in a pink halter top and poom poom shorts. The baby pink looked good against her dark chocolate complexion. Her new braids were bunched in a ponytail, revealing her new gold hoops with her name on them. She's been rocking them since she got them for her birthday back in May. Gold always looks good on people of the darker persuasion. It's something about the way it glistens on their beige, amaretto, caramel, chocolate, and blue-black skin. The shine of the metal accentuates their God-given gift of color. But I didn't know why she wore her newest prize possession today, we weren't going anywhere but on this here stoop.

"Why you got on your new hoops?" I had said to her.

"You never know who might stroll by."

"Girl, Junior has already seen your new hoops."

"I know," she had said with a sly smile. "But he said he likes the way my neck looks with them on."

"Shit. You better watch it," I had told her. "Junior's liable to be kissing that neck one night and your new gold be gone."

"Please, Junior would never steal from me."

I then told her, "Junior would steal milk from his momma!"

"Naw, he's just a charmer. He charms his way into getting those things with his big almond eyes."

"Whatever. Keep believing that and you'll end up earless just 'cause he couldn't get the latches undone quick enough!"

I swear that girl is so in love with Junior that she can't see him for what he is—a lying thief with an addictive habit. He could use his smarts for shoplifting for so much more. He could make a killing if he opened up a shop. No, he's just a two-bit thief who enjoys the high from not getting caught. I guess he could be getting high off something else, like that crack they're talking about that just hit the streets. But I can't say none of that to Mel. That's her man. And he can't do no wrong.

Now, back to this bourgeois sister. I have to calm down, 'cause I think that prep school bitch is harping on the fact that I'm white. All the new folks do.

* * *

Moving day, and from what I can scope out, this family has a lot of stuff. All of it ain't fitting in that apartment. And Ms. Prissy sure ain't getting all those shoes in that box marked SHOES under her bed.

"You think they rich?" Mel asks as one of the movers pushes us aside to get in the door.

"Naw, what would they be moving here for?"

"Well, they sure got a lot of stuff."

"Yeah."

I can feel someone looking at me when I turn to see Mel staring at my neck.

"What?"

"You forgot to put on your sunblock," she whispers.

To my amazement, I do feel the tingling sensation of sunburn approaching.

"I'll be back."

I take the stairs because the movers have the elevator tied up. I left my sunblock on the bed without putting it on. White skin turns red in the sun, so I have to keep sunblock on in the summer. Just so I won't look like a dried-up beet. I don't know what I was thinking about. I always put on my UV ray protection. I go all the way to Macy's on 34th to get it. Yeah, it doesn't bother me to be white, but it's a bitch to deal with sunburn!

As I strip to apply my secret remedy for summer, I take a glance in the mirror. My 5'7" frame is still skinny regardless of all those White Castle burgers we eat. I love the way my blondish-brown hair kisses my shoulders. The highlights from the sun really bring out my hair's natural shine. My mom says I remind her of that 70s supermodel, Bo Dereck. She says I have her height, the legs, the hair and the attitude. All I need are the breasts. I'm starting to think my lumps won't ever develop. Seems like forever that I've been waiting. Shoot, I just got a training bra last year. Mel got hers at 12. I'll never get titties and hips like her. That's just DNA. But I work with what I have. I can fit my size six into anything and look like I'm straight off the cover of *Teen Magazine*. I smile at myself. A product of my mom keeping in touch with a Yonkers orthodontist. I turn to the side to get a glimpse of my butt. Yep, it's good. Not fat, but plump. The guys will love that this summer when I rock my biker shorts and sports bra. Other than needing a tan, I look like any other Latina American. That's what most people think I am. Either that or mixed. I don't care what they say, but right now I'm paler than Casper and need some sun. I put back on my denim shorts and white t-shirt. It's too hot for socks and sneakers but going barefoot through this building will have you being admitted to the hospital for heroine use or this AIDS thing. Needles are all over the place. Especially on the weekends, the working man's holiday.

I race out of my room, but then decide to grab my hair gel, rubber bands, a comb and a brush. I remember that I also need a Tupperware dish full of water. Mel doesn't know it, but she is about to spend the next few hours braiding my hair. Look out, Bo!

When I get back downstairs, Melinda isn't on the stoop. I look up and down the block, but I don't see her anywhere. I figure she had to go inside to use the bathroom or something when Mrs. Wendell yells out the window.

"She went around the corner with that fool Junior Moore. Told her he got some new stuff he wanted her to see, maybe give her something from his run last night."

Nosy Mrs. Wendell would know that. Every community has one. A snoop, an instigator. A middle-aged, lonely, busybody who sticks her head out the window all day, every day. Just watching and spying. Taking in all the information she can. But they never use the knowledge for good, just gossip. Mrs. Wendell and I have a love-hate relationship. I love her when she gives me the scoop on sales at the Food Lion or at a department store. I love her for not complaining about the smoke from the barbecue grill I keep on the fire escape. Just give her a steak and she keeps her mouth shut to the landlord. But there have been more times than I can count when I hate her for telling my mom when we sneak in late. That woman can't wait to spill the beans. And that's what she would get. Moms would give her beans, sugar, eggs, anything she needed as a reward for telling her what I did. Since Moms is working when I am usually creeping, Mrs. Wendell is her eyes and ears.

"Said she'd be right back."

"Thanks, Mrs. Wendell."

I sit down and start to brush my hair to get it ready for Mel.

Mrs. Wendell says, "I guess our new neighbors are finished unloading."

I didn't notice there weren't any movers asking me to move within the last ten seconds.

I ask, because I know she knows, "What's their name?"

"Stevens. I hear they come from Stamford, Connecticut."

"What they doing here?"

"I hear the woman's husband left her for a white woman. Won't pay her child support and she never worked a day in her life. I guess that's why she's here. The girl's about your age, you should talk to her."

I ain't talking to nobody. This is my territory, people speak to me, I think to myself.

But before I can reply, here comes Mel running down the block, up the steps and past me. She mumbles something that sounds like "be back." And then she's gone. I wonder what is in that shopping bag she nearly hits me with when she whizzes by me. Two minutes later, she is sitting down next to me, smiling.

"Huh, huh. What did Junior give you now?" I say all too

THE OTHER SIDE OF DA COURT

knowingly.

"What he gave us."

"What do you mean?"

Mel leans over me to see if Mrs. Wendell is still in the window. She is.

"Hi, Mrs. Wendell."

"Hmph!" the Hawk says and backs away from the window, probably to get something to drink.

"Nosy!" Turning her attention back to me, Mel says, "Junior lifted Moddell's Sporting Goods Store last night. That's why he wasn't at the party. My man was scheming and cleaning them out!"

"What did he get?" I ask, a little bit anxiously.

It surprises me because I'm usually not phased when Junior gives her stuff. I usually scold her for taking hot items. And sometimes, when Junior's running from the law, he asks her to hide stuff in her house! I tell her she's going to get caught one day. She ignores me and sports whatever jewelry or clothes he gives her for hiding his lifted goods.

She claims her rewards are paid for. I just laugh. She can believe what she wanna! But Mel's even taken aback by my curiosity. I guess she saw my ears perk up when she said "us."

"He got us some biker shorts and two pairs of new kicks each!"

Then I notice her ponytail was no longer there. Her hair barrette was around her wrist and her braids were hanging down.

"And he gave you an ugly hickey!" I say, disgusted, as I lift her hair up.

She swats my hand away with a smile. Fast ass, I think. I'm sorry, I ain't giving it up no time soon. I'm not going to end up alone and pregnant like Stacy, Mercedes and Lakisha. Girls from my crew that got knocked up by some idiots from around the way and now live up in the women's shelter. I don't know why they call it a women's shelter, mostly teenagers occupy it.

No, I'm saving my goods for real love. I'm a product of real love so I know what it's about.

My mom loved my dad so much that she married him. Left her

19

high-paying nursing job and dreams of becoming a doctor in Connecticut to be with him, here in the Boogie Down. That's love. I'm not saying I'll go from riches to rags for some man, but I do know if someone loves you, and you them, you might give up your place of residence, but never your integrity. Mel hasn't learned that yet. She looks like the slut of the day with that hickey. But I will admit, I'm jealous. Not of the love mark, because there are other places where a hickey can go not for all the world to see. But I'm envious that she has found someone whom she *thinks* she can have a future with. Sometimes, I wish my knight in shining armor would appear as well.

"So what do you want to do with your hair?" she asks.

"Just cornrow it all back."

"Like every summer?"

"Yeah."

* * *

The hotter it gets, the harder it gets to breathe. My hair is done and I'm Bo Dereck's younger sister once again. Mel reminds me to have her do it every week, unlike last year when I let it go two weeks and it was a bitch to untangle.

Sirens can be heard all over the city from our spot on the stoop. I guess that's what makes me think about what's hot for tonight.

"So what we getting into tonight, girl?" Mel musta read my mind. We do that sometimes.

"I thought you were chilling; 'cause you got caught last night."

"I didn't get caught," Mel whispers. But I know differently. Mel might live two floors down, but project walls are thin.

"I don't know, you hear about anything going down?"

Mel sighs. "Naw. We should go down to da court. There's always talk about the hot spots down there."

She's right. Anytime we want a handle on who's throwing a party, who's using their fake ID to go to the club, who got shot, or who's up in juvey hall, we go to the basketball court down the street. That's how we found out about last night's house party.

"What time is it?"

Mrs. Wendell says, "Almost one."

"Shit!" I yell. "I gotta make my mother lunch. She'll be home in a half hour."

Moms works on Saturdays too. But she has Sundays and Monday mornings off. So I fix her a big lunch Saturday afternoons, the good daughter I am. Saturday is also her payday. That's when I get my allowance for all the hard work I do. I get more than my friends get. Even though money is tight, Moms more than compensates me for taking care of the cooking, cleaning, and laundry of the house. Hmph, makes me mad sometimes. I do all the work but it is *her* house when I get in trouble.

Saturdays are also her working man's holiday, like everyone else in these parts. All Moms wants on the weekends is food in the fridge and a full stock of rum. So I keep a well-loaded freezer. She provides the liquor. Since Pops died, Bacardi has become her companion. She spends so many Saturdays and Sundays with Mr. Bacardi, she never knows what I am up to. I'll come home at 3 a.m. and she's in a drunken stupor on the couch, hugged up with Mr. Bacardi or Captain Morgan, or whoever was cheap that night for a date. That's why on the weekends I have my freedom. Moms doesn't know the half unless Mrs. Wendell spills the beans. That's why I keep three of everything, always one for Mrs. Wendell.

I pull my stuff together to go upstairs and cook. Just then, Mel's mom calls out the window. "Meliiiiiiiiiinnnnnnnnddddddaaaaaaaaaa!" The sound sends chills up our spines.

"Oh, oh."

"Girl, you didn't clean your room while I went to the grocery store?"

"Naw. I just chilled and waited for you. Besides, my mom wasn't paying me no mind. Freddie stopped by early this morning. He's probably fixing to leave, that's why she noticed I wasn't around."

Ms. Green is all over Mel about her behavior and chores until Freddie stops by. All disciplining in the Green household ceases when our faithful, sweet garbage man Freddie Meyers saunters in with takeout in one hand and condoms in the other. Ms. Green thinks Freddie is going to make Department of Sanitation supervisor some day and move them into the suburbs. So all her attention goes on Freddie.

"Well, I gotta go make lunch for my mom."

"I gotta go clean my room."

"Let's meet back here at five. We'll head down to da court and get some word about tonight."

"Yep. How much you think we'll need? I gotta hit Freddie up before he leaves."

"I'm thinking forty dollars."

"Forty?! I just hit him up for fifty dollars last Wednesday. I told him I saw a pair of kicks I wanted. I spent that on my outfit for last night."

That's the thing about house parties, all you need is five dollars to get in, but you can't go up in there with last week's outfit. Same neighborhood, same stores, same outfit in three different colors. You'll see yourself twice in one night if you don't spend the dough on a new outfit. You'll get your feelings hurt too 'cause folks are quick to call you out. I usually get one hundred twenty dollars every week, so I'm straight. Mel thinks I'm rich. We would be if our money didn't go to Chin Foo's Liquor Depot every week. Then Moms could fulfill her dream and move like she wants. I'd stay put with my girls and my savings. I love my mom, but I'm no dummy. I always put away something for a rainy day. And I guess it's raining on Melinda.

"Get what you can, I'll front the rest."

"Bet," Melinda smiles. "See you at five."

Upstairs, I stand in front of the fridge debating what to make for my moms. It's too hot to use the oven. Then I remember the hot dogs I bought this morning. I open the kitchen window that leads out onto the fire escape and heat up the grill. On the menu today is grilled hot dogs and my famous potato salad. I can throw down on some salad. Everyone says so. Actually, most people rave about my cooking. I have to admit, I like creating meals and having folks roll out of their chairs with smiles on their faces. But today, I'm keeping it simple. I put the potatoes on and cleaned up the kitchen from last night. Me and Mel threw down on some Philly steaks I made. We needed a hearty meal to absorb the liquor we intended to drink at the party. Just as I started mixing the potatoes, Moms walks in. Her face, drawn. Eyes, sunken. She is exhausted.

"Hi," she says with a sigh.

"Hi. How was work?"

"Fine." She comes into the kitchen to see what contraption I'm cooking up. And to set her two bottles of Coke in the fridge. From another bag, she reveals the largest bottle possible of Bacardi and places it in the pantry.

As she gets closer to me, I steal a glimpse of her face. Her shoulder-length, honey-suckle hair is pulled into a bun, exposing her high cheekbones and European nose. Her freckles are showing today because of the sun. But her arms are almost radish red. Moms isn't concerned about sunburn. If you had to travel an hour to and from work, no matter what the season, you wouldn't care either. Just that you needed to get to work and make money to survive.

Moms leaves the kitchen at a slow pace, unpinning her hair as she walks down the hall. In her day, she was the prize of Connecticut: dance, piano, boarding school, tennis. She had beauty and brains. She told me one interested beau called her a cross between Jackie Kennedy and Cheryl Tiegs. She was a woman with daring, sexy looks who could charm the pants off of a president. Well, she chose no president, just a teacher with dreams. My mom loved my dad's drive. She enjoyed his rebellious way of thinking out of the norm. Now, the Bronx wasn't her ideal place to raise a family but then again, for her, Connecticut was so boring. Especially for a woman who wanted to experience life. Life had treated her well until Pops died. She was the white princess of the Bronx. Everyone thought she and Pops were royalty. They were loved and respected in the community. They weren't just weekend do-gooders who looked at the residents like charity cases. No, they were residents themselves. That made an impact in the neighborhood. But ever since August 10, 1982, her crown has slipped. And now she's just another Bronxite trying to make a living. Hoping to leave one day. I feel sorry for her. She's let herself go. Her butt's getting saggy, her chest is already there and she never wears makeup anymore. I remember when I used to play with her make-up as a little girl. She would say, "Now, you can only use last year's colors." Now, last year's colors are seven years gone and in the trash.

After a lukewarm bath, Mom returns from her bedroom down the hall in a t-shirt and shorts. Her meal done, she sits at the dinette set by the kitchen window, ready to be served.

"Where's the mail?"

I retrieve it from the table near the front door and hand it to her as she stuffs her face. She may be out of it but she knows that a few days after school lets out, report cards are in the mail. I have nothing to worry about. She leans on me hard when it comes to studying. That's all she asks of me. So to make my life easier, and my pockets heavier, I keep my grades up. She finds what she's looking for and opens the brown envelope with a return address that reads Albert Lehman High School. Like clockwork, she smiles as she reads off my As and Bs. I did get a C+ in science. Probably because I cursed out old man Mitchell for giving us that pop quiz on the elements back in April. I told him he was an asshole for not warning us. He gave me three days' detention and hasn't liked me ever since. Hey, I only told the truth. This C+ must be my punishment. Moms doesn't mind. Not everyone can excel in science like she did. So she pulls my allowance out of her bosom. And I follow suit and place it in mine. With a kiss, I leave the kitchen and run to my room. I have a few stashes of savings so a thief could easily be tripped up. I put this wad of loot into my don't-know-what-I'm-going-to-do-after-high-school money. I'll use it for whatever I decide to do after I get my diploma. With over two grand, me and Mel can get an apartment and jobs as secretaries in Manhattan. That's our tentative plan. I set aside money for tonight and a little extra for my ace.

From out in the kitchen, I hear the dishes clank in the sink and the squeak of the pantry door opening. It won't be long before Moms is on her date.

I go out to the kitchen and clean up. Checking the time, it's only a little after three. Two hours to kill. Moms takes her usual seat on the couch and picks up the phone. Every week she calls my Aunt Trudy in Bridgeport. They fill each other in on the goings on in the upper class sector. I hear Mom say she can't wait until July 4th for the annual family picnic and boat ride. I dread it. I tune the rest of the conversation out and try to think of what I can wear tonight.

"There's more potato salad in the fridge. And I made up ham and cheese wedges for you." I inform her once she hangs up the phone. She's like a baby when she drinks, needs everything within her reach. I cross in front of the TV and turn on the window fan.

"Did you get my chips and dip?"

"Yes."

"And my cheese danish for breakfast?"

I don't even know why she asks. "Yes."

The phone rings. Again like clockwork, it's Loretta. Mom's drinking buddy from two doors down. Loretta is Mom's only friend. They sit around and shoot the shit. And *if* my mother decides to leave the block, for reasons other than work, it's Loretta who goes with her. They chill all weekend drinking and eating and laughing. Loretta used to teach with Pops. So they go way back. She'll be over in a few and their double date will commence.

I spot the time; it's standing still. I can't leave until Moms is good and lit. Three drinks after Loretta comes over and they won't know I'm gone. In my room, I glance in my closet for some gear to wear down to da court. Even though we're just going down the block, we have to look good. All the honeys will be down there, running ball or hanging out. Last week I bought a one-piece spandex short set. Its sleeveless, blue and white material clings to me like chewing gum to new kicks. Speaking of new sneakers, I wonder what kind Junior lifted for us. The new Reeboks are hype. Oh well, for now, I'll just put on my solid white ones. After a good bird bath in the sink, the clock strikes 4 p.m. Not long now, I apply more sunblock. I put my chain on, the one that says "Le-Le" in Chinese block letters. I just bought a two-finger ring that matches. Mel hasn't seen it yet. She

25

thinks she has one on me with her new hoops, but she is mistaken. I am going to bust out with my ring, a ring that mostly guys are wearing. But I like it and I don't pay attention to barriers. Besides, I hear they come in handy in a fight. This girl, Stephanie, still has Tasha's name slightly embedded in her jaw from their fight last month!

Fully clothed and looking cute, I spot the time, 4:35. I can't wait any longer. Besides, Loretta is here and I can sneak out.

"Lisa." Damn, I'm caught.

"Yes."

"Where are you going in that slut suit?"

"It's not a slut suit and I'm going to da court."

"Be back in this house by nine."

"Yes." Shit. I'll be back, but I won't be staying.

On my way down the stairs, I hear yelling. As I get closer to the third floor, I realize that's Ms. Green's voice filling the hallways. I debate whether or not I should knock on the door. She might be killing Melinda. But I decide not to. In this neighborhood, sometimes you just need to mind your business.

I sit on the stoop waiting for Mel. It's ten after five. I don't think she's coming. Before I can finish my thought, Mel walks out the door. She's in one piece but she looks vexed.

"What's up?"

"Report cards came today."

"Yep, I know."

"I've got to report to summer school Monday morning."

"Damn!"

"My mom's trippin'!"

"Was it bad?"

"What? My mom or my grades?"

"Both."

"Yeah."

"How bad?"

"I don't want to talk about it. The only reason why she stopped yelling long enough for me to leave is because Freddie called from a pay phone."

"I thought he was here."

"With my mom yelling like that? Naw. He left a little while ago to get movies, food and liquor. He called because he forgot to ask her what she was drinking tonight. I slipped out while she was sweet-talking him."

"What are you going to do?"

"What do you mean? I'm going out. Shit, this is my last weekend before I head to summer school. I'ma have fun tonight."

"What about getting dressed later?"

"She won't notice when I come back, Freddie will be back by then."

We start to walk down the street to da court. We pass other project buildings. Most are run down with broken windows. The only houses on the block are across the street. In their hey day, they were the brownstones to the rich. Now, they're worthless structures of brick being held up only by the surrounding scaffolding. Some realtor is remodeling them to sell. Who in their right mind would buy them? As we approach the corner, a quick right takes us into the entrance of the park. Mad folks are out with their bikes, radios, and kids. Just trying to beat the heat.

Our destination is the heart of the park, the pulse of the neighborhood. Da court is where everything of importance happens. It's the Wall Street of this hood. Many a' drug sales, love affairs, fights and block parties take place right here. You want to know something, come to da court and you'll find that out and then some.

We sit on the sidelines watching a game. Charlie, Juan, Eric, and Shadow give us a nod, but keep playing. They are our male counterparts. Our running buddies. These guys know how to throw down. Them, Mel and I, plus Deadre and Myra, hang out in school and around the way. Deadre and Myra have part-time jobs on Saturdays. So they hook up with us at night. When the game is over, the guys come over and sit with us.

"What's up y'all?" Eric the jokester says.

"Nuttin'."

"So, Mel, you get balled out last night?" She knew that was coming from him. She just sucks her teeth. My eye is on a group of girls playing double dutch on the tennis court. Folks 'round here don't know nothing about tennis. But we do know the court makes the best site for a double-dutch tournament. I am concentrating on one girl's turn when Shadow comes up behind me and hugs me.

"What's up, girl?" Shadow is the affectionate one. Always sharing, lending an ear or shoulder to cry on. Sometimes Juan and Charlie, the tough guys, rag on him for being "sweet." But they've used that shoulder to cry on too, so it doesn't phase Shadow one bit.

"What's hot for tonight?" I ask them.

"We were going to chill at Eric's crib. He's got a/c," Charlie says. This is obviously news to Eric by the grimace on his face.

"Naw, man. My mom is babysitting my niece." Ever since Eric's brother died in that gang shootout last year, his mother takes care of the baby Emilio had with Sandra from Brooklyn.

"C'mon, y'all. Me and Le-Le wanna go out," Mel whines.

Shadow notices my ring. "Why, so you can get ganked for your ring?"

All eyes turn to my hands. Words of approval rise from all angles. Mel likes it but I know what she's thinking. "Heifer's been holding out, gotta get me one."

Just then, some brothers yell over and ask if the guys are done with the court. Six tall brothers with athletic bodies start to warm up. One in particular catches my eye. I've never seen him before. Must be new to the hood. His medium brown body lunges after a layup with perfection. His low-cut fade accentuates his ebony eyes and small nose. I can tell he can kiss from the full lips he licks as he gets warmed up. This light-skinned dude yells to him, "X, you got defense." So "X" is his name. I have got to find out more about him. Mel must have read my mind 'cause she blatantly yells over to them, "Where y'all from?"

"X" turns and says, "We're from Syracuse University. We're freshmen in basketball camp, training for the upcoming season."

So he's a college man. Nice. I'd school him any day!

He catches my eye and I give him my *Teen* magazine smile to say, "Hi, will you marry me?"

By the way he keeps looking even after his boy almost hits him with the ball, I know I've got him. Before I leave, those digits and lips are mine.

"Awright, y'all, c'mon, what's up?" Charlie says to bring me back from my fantasy.

"We could hit the club."

"Naw."

"We could cool out here in the park." We all look at Eric and think, he must be out his mind! Over half the population in a four-block radius has been raped, mugged or shot up in this park after dark. No thank you.

"Well, I wasn't going to say anything, but my parents left for down south this morning. I've got the house to myself for the night," Shadow offers, since there is nothing else going on.

"Bet. Y'all get the liquor, we'll bring the food," Melinda schemes. Knowing damn well she didn't get the chance to hit Freddie up for some dough. That means it's up to me to buy the munchies and hope Deadre and Myra show up to pay me their share.

At that, we agree to meet at Shadow's around 8 p.m. We promise to clean up afterwards 'cause his aunt from White Plains is coming down in the morning to Shadow-sit for the next two weeks.

We all get up to leave da court, when I hear someone say, "Excuse me." I turn to see "X" running over to us. He sets his eyes on me and asks if he can talk to me for a second. I smile nonchalantly and saunter out of earshot of my friends.

"How you doing?"

"Fine and you?"

"Not as fine as you." He knew it was a line and I wasn't biting. So I roll my eyes.

"All right, that was corny. Forgive me. But I had to say something to you. My name is Xavier, what's yours?" That explains the "X."

"I'm Lisa, Le-Le for short." I shoot his fine ass a smile and bat my eyes.

"You from around here?"

"Yeah. You're not. Where you from?"

"Originally Virginia." That also explains the southern drawl. "But I've lived in Harlem for the last five years."

"Damn. Harlem. You're a long way from home."

"Yeah, I'm a freshmen at Syracuse U., starting in September. We're training now. One of my boys lives around here and we're chillin' with him this weekend. Summer housing opens on Monday."

"Oh, so you're a college man."

"Yeah. How old are you?"

"Why, do I look like jail bait?"

"Honestly? You look good enough to serve two sentences! But how old *are* you?

"Fifteen. You?"

"Seventeen. I'll be 18 in August. Well, your friends look like they're about to leave you. Can I ask you for your number?"

"I don't know, do you think you're worthy of my number?"

He smiles. Perfect, shy. And a bit naughty. But that is good. He is forward and a gentleman. I like that. I like him.

"Well, I'd like to prove myself worthy." I like his answer, too. So I give him my number. He promises to call me Sunday around two. We'll see. These shady brothers are all talk, no action.

On the way home, we stop at the corner store for chips, cookies and penny candy, just cause Mel wants them. Wedge rolls and cold cuts. All to get ready for a night of eating and drinking at Shadow's.

CHAPTER TWO

Horizontal lines of sunlight filter in through the apartment. I roll over to keep from completely waking up and bumping into something. Or somebody. Before the sunshine could fully wake me, the nausea in my stomach rouses me with a jolt. My eyes pop open and my only thought is to get to the bathroom, fast. But when I jump up to make a run for it, I trip. Not a clear path in sight. If it's not a sleeping body in my way, empty liquor bottles clutter my route. I take the short cut and climb over the coffee table, holding my mouth, knowing any extra movement would cause my stomach to turn against me. Just as my hand can't hold my cheeks anymore, I reach the bathroom. There, I make friends with Shadow's toilet. It's a cool and understanding companion in my time of need. In between heaves, I promise that I won't drink ever again. But come next week, that promise will be long forgotten. I can't help it. I like to drink. I mean, shit, alcohol is a bitch coming up; but it's smooth going down. And you know, we're not supposed to consume it at our age. But defiance makes any drink or act sweeter.

With the rumbling in my stomach the only evidence of last night's shot contest, me and Mel leave Shadow's around 8:30 a.m. She looks how I feel as we head home. I don't know if it's the Absolut and BBQ corn chips repeating on her, or worry of what will be waiting for her at home, that has Mel's face frozen with agony. I would tell her she can crash at my place but I don't for two reasons. One, she's got to go home sometime. And two, I want to fucking sleep! So I keep my suggestion to myself and keep walking in silence. I do say a short prayer that my friend will live to hear the summer school bell ring come tomorrow morning.

Sleep comes easy when you're hungover. I don't know why, but as soon as your head hits the pillow, you're out. But it's a dreamless and restless sleep, waking up still very much exhausted. I'm used to it though. We do this every weekend. Partying is our favorite past time. There's nothing like friends, food, and liquor to get the party started. I think America should lower the drinking age. The government wants to raise it to 21. I think they're full of shit. Statistics show most accidents happen while drivers are under the influence. And by raising the legal age to purchase alcohol, there's a better chance that the more responsible adult won't drive drunk. Well, if the drinking age was my age, the government wouldn't have to worry. Kids my age don't always drive! I never heard of a WWI—Walking While Intoxicated—have you?

Suddenly, a loud noise wakes me from my drunken sleep. I can't differentiate where it's coming from, but damn, I wish it would stop. I open my eyes only after smelling the sweet staleness of Coke. My mom is standing over me, looking half asleep herself. She hands me the phone. Who the hell?

"Hello?!"

"May I speak to Le-Le, please?"

"Who's this?" My friends know not to call me this early after a night of heavy partying.

"My name is Xavier. I met her at the park yesterday."

Bam! Ain't nothing like a phone call from a cutie to cure a hangover. Sobriety is necessary when flirting, or you could get yourself in trouble.

"Oh, hey, how you doing?" I say as I try to sit up in bed. The walls slightly start to spin.

"I'm fine. Can you talk? Did I catch you at a bad time? I did say I would call you later on."

"No, it's straight. What time is it anyway?"

"Almost noon."

"Oh."

"Was that your dad who answered the phone?"

"No, my mom." I wanted to laugh but my head hurt so I keep the joke to myself. Moms does sound like a dude when she's drunk. She's probably pissed about the phone waking her up, too. When I came in last night after da court to change, she and Loretta were knocked out already. And this morning, they were in the same spot. Let me tell you, ain't nothing like the shrill of the phone to make you rise from a drunken stupor. I'm kind of vexed too, but then I remember how cute this guy is. So I keep my curses to myself.

"So how you doing today?"

"Okay." I'm trying not to focus on the ceiling that is closing in on me.

"That's good. So tell me about yourself."

"What do you want to know?"

"Everything."

"You first," I say, buying myself time to take the cordless phone into the bathroom and wash my face.

"Well, like I said, I'm 17 and a freshmen at S.U. I won a basketball scholarship so I'm thankful to be in college right now. My major is business only because they say it will come in handy to manage my own affairs once I'm in the NBA. All I want to do is ball, but education is important, too. I mean when I've reached my prime, what am I going to do? Shrivel up and die? I could easily do that if I couldn't ball anymore. But reality tells me I better have something to fall back on. I'm sorry, am I talking too much?"

"Naw." Yeah, he is, but it gives me time to pull myself together.

"People say I can run my mouth. They say it's the country boy in me. I tell them the media will like a ball player who can express his feelings off the court. So what's up with you? Tell me about Le-Le."

"Well, I'm 15 and I go to Lehman."

"What are you into?"

"What do you mean?"

"Like I'm into balling, what are your hobbies?"

"Hanging with my crew, going to parties and drinking."

"Do you do anything after school?"

"Yeah, my homework, the cooking, the cleaning and the

laundry."

"Wow. I meant do you belong to any clubs?"

"Hell no! Clubs are whack!"

"You say it like it's a bad thing. A requirement of admission to most colleges is to have some type of extra-curricular activities."

"I'm not planning on going to college." He is starting to get on my nerves.

"Why not? You can't do anything without a degree. What do you want to be?"

"I don't know, never thought about it."

"Well you're only 15. You have time to decide."

What the hell is he talking about? I have time. Time for what? I don't plan on "being" anything. I just want to live. Why are he and my guidance counselor so bent out of shape over my plans for the future? Just 'cause I don't exactly have a plan doesn't mean I'll be some low-life on the street. Shit. He is starting to piss me off.

"So you like to party? What's your curfew?"

"Curfew, I don't have one of those."

"Why not?"

"My mom is usually asleep when I go out so I come and go as I please," I lied. Sleep perhaps, an intoxicated coma, definitely.

"Oh, so you're a rebel. You think you're grown."

"I am grown," I say with as much attitude as I can muster up.

"Okay, okay. I'm just messing with you. So listen, I'm heading upstate tomorrow. Summer housing is opening. But I would like to see you again before I leave."

I don't know if I want to see this brother. He woke me up. Called my mother a man. And made me feel like the scum of the earth because I don't know what I'd like to "be." Fuck him! He can take my number and shove it!

"Well, can I see you? Talk to you face to beautiful face?"

I know I am in trouble because my attitude flips a script at the word "beautiful."

"Sure, I can see you. We can meet in the park at three. Cool?"

"Cool. I can't wait to see you, my Puerto Rican princess." And he hangs up.

Damn! The brother just doesn't know! With my sleep pattern broken, I can't return to my coma. My stomach's doing something weird, too. I can't tell if it's the leftover alcohol or hunger. I know it's not butterflies over this brother. He doesn't even know me! He doesn't even know what I am! How is he just going to assume I'm Rican. I could be mixed, Brazilian, Mexican or Dominican. Oh, the Dominicans hate that. Shit, you better hide if you call a group of Dominicans Puerto Rican. That's shameful to them. It's fighting words. Same with blacks. Some prefer to be called black. Others this "African-American" shit someone just started. But don't call them Jamaican or Haitian. It's like all hell broke loose. It's like talking about their momma! I don't understand this classification shit. I mean Hispanic is Hispanic and black is black. Sure, our origin of birth is different, but this caste system of color, complexion and culture should invoke pride. Not be a dividing line. I'm white. It doesn't matter if my family is a French and Italian mix. Regardless, I'm white and that's that. Why must we classify each other by race anyway? Flesh is flesh and blood is blood. Why can't we just be people, a people of mixed heritages with a common goal to get along? Makes me mad. But if you're going to classify each other, get it right. Damn!

Two o'clock. Sleep deprived and vexed, I'm trying to decide if I still want to meet Xavier. But the determining factor remains the same: he's cute! I jump up in an instant, forgetting about my hangover. Peppermint tea and a shower will cure that. Sober and clean, my dressing ritual doesn't take long. I apply my sunblock while debating on my choice of outfits. I think I'm going to go with the grey tank top with my Levi overall shorts. Damn, I wish I would remember to get those new kicks from Mel. I lace up my grey and white Nikes at three on the dot. Keys in hand, I'm out.

"Where you going?" Moms says as she's mealing on a wedge.

"To da court."

"Bring me a bottle of Coke when you come back."

"I thought you brought home two bottles yesterday."

"You still here?"

Moms don't talk to me much. She doesn't ask for much either. But when she does, she tries to command respect. I listen to her. I love and respect her because she's my mom. But I do for her out of pity. See, Pops took care of her. And now that she doesn't care enough about herself, it's my job to take care of her. I guess you could say our roles have been reversed. It's cool though. I don't mind. But sometimes I wonder: will I ever have to be taken care of? Then reality kicks in, Le-Le can take care of Le-Le, she doesn't need anybody.

My stride is quick but calculated. A woman can't be too anxious, it turns a brother off. But so does being late, so I power walk down the street. Along the way, I take in my hood. The sun's rays have brought folks out on the stoop. Old Man Thomas and Ms. Ellie sit in their folding chairs. Their radio is playing some oldies but goodies station as they sip on homemade lemonade. Mr. Thomas is known for his lemonade, since way back when he was a boy in Georgia. He usually makes huge tubs of it when we have our Labor Day block party. Most come from 10 blocks over to get a taste. I could use some now, but it'll have to wait. I keep steppin'. Ray Ray and 'em are shooting craps by the curb.

"What's up, y'all?" I yell over their bickering.

"'Sup, Le!" they say in unison, never turning away from the game. You never take your eyes off your money pile. You'll be a broke brother when you look back down.

At the corner, I cross the street and enter the park. I stroll the rest of the way until I reach the heart of our communication center. Da court is jumpin' today. Brothers are balling big time. It looks like the NBA draft up in here.

"Le-Le."

I turn and Xavier walks towards me from the sidelines of an intense game. I wait patiently, at least my body does, my heart's going crazy.

"Hi."

"Hi."

"Do you wanna grab a bench in the park?"

"Okay."

We walk in silence. I glance at him from the corner of my eye. There's something about him that I can't explain. I don't know him, hell, I'm almost mad at him, yet I'm excited to be near him. It's like I anticipate something from him, but what?

We stop at a bench at the corner of the park. To my right is a botanical garden blooming with foreign and domestic flowers. It's beautiful the way our view enables us to see every inch of the garden. Their colors remind me of the first day of art class when Mrs. Tameki showed us the universal color spectrum. How we can make one color from two others. It's amazing. But these species look like their colors weren't mixed with paint, but by nature's evolution. I never noticed the garden before.

"Is this bench okay?" he asks just as sure as day.

I think he planned it, the spot is too perfect. "Yeah, it's cool," I admit nonchalantly. Not wanting to show my awe at the beauty he placed before me.

"So how you doing?"

"Good. I'm kind of tired. A few of us chilled last night at my friend Shadow's house."

"Is that the one who was hugging on you yesterday?"

"Yeah." Do I hear a twinge of jealousy in that question?

"I thought he was your man for a minute. But he let me talk to you so I knew it was cool."

Damn, he was scoping me out like that?

"What did y'all do?"

"Chilled. Got some liquor and I made us some food."

"You cook?"

"Yep, damn good, too."

"All right, all right. You have to cook for me one day."

"Maybe." I give him my *Teen* magazine smile with my *Right On* magazine attitude.

"So how do y'all get liquor if y'all are only 15?"

"Eric and Charlie are the only ones my age, plus Melinda. But Shadow and my girls Myra and Deadre are 17. And besides, Crazy

Man Watts sells alcohol to anybody."

"Crazy Man Watts? Who's that?"

"He lives in the basement of a building on my block. He's supposed to be the super for the building. But his time is spent on his money-maker: booze. He'll sell it to anyone. If you paying, you drinking. He's a little messed up from his Vietnam days so you have to proceed with caution when you knock on his door. Once he came at these brothers with a butter knife, making gun noises. Screaming, 'You dead, Charlie, how you like my M-80!'"

We both laugh hysterically.

"Yeah, he's a trip," I say, reminiscing.

"We had a dude in Virginia that sold to minors. Didn't care about anybody."

"I don't know 'bout that. Nobody remembers how Mr. Watts was before he went crazy from that Red Orange shit. I just know he's where my peep's get our liquor from. He's the fucking Motel 6 for the neighborhood alkies. Always got his light on."

"You curse a lot, don't you?"

"What do you mean?"

"I mean a girl as pretty as you shouldn't curse like a dude."

"What does it matter to you?"

"I just say what I feel."

"Then feel this, you 'bout to piss me off. You pissed me off on the phone and now we were just having a good conversation."

"How did I piss you off on the phone?"

"Making me feel like shit. I mean bad, for not having plans for the future."

"You gotta have plans if you want to be something."

"Why do I have to *be* something? Why can't I just live?"

"Live and do what?"

"Live and hang out with my friends."

"How will you provide for yourself?"

"Me and Mel got that figured out. We're taking typing in school now. We'll get jobs as secretaries and get an apartment together. I've already got money saved towards the crib after we graduate from high school."

"Anybody can answer a phone and type. Don't you want more for yourself?"

I hadn't thought about it that way.

"Don't you want to do something important with your life? Be somebody who can say I accomplished this. Raise yourself out of the community but be wealthy enough to give back to your roots? Why do you just want to exist?"

"'Cause if you become someone too important people look at you differently. You're not one of them; you're above them. They'll shoot you down. Dowse all that seniority with a bullet to the neck!"

"Bullet to the neck?"

I hadn't realized I said it. I try to avoid it. I try to let it slide.

"So you're saying if you just exist, or co-exist within your environment, you'll survive. You'll lead a happy life, never exceeding yours and their expectations."

"Yeah, something like that." I get tight lipped.

"Don't close up, talk to me."

"What?! What do you want from me!" I scream. Not realizing I had jumped up from my seat. "If you try to raise up higher than what people expect, they'll shoot you down. You're just another idiot with a dream in these parts. Be dead by morning if you even act like you can do better!" I shout. "Look at all those folks who tried to do something for others, who tried to be somebody. Martin, Malcolm, my pops...they're just dead somebodies!"

It was out before I knew it. Xavier is looking at me like he'd never laid eyes on me yesterday. He steps towards me and hugs me like it is his last request as a dying man.

"So that's it," he whispers as he holds me tighter.

I wonder what he means. Then it hit me. I am crying. I hear my sobs. I feel the warm flow of salty tears against my cheeks. I am crying. Le-Le doesn't cry! This brother has brought me here and I never realized it. I am angry. Angry because I never really cried over my pops. Everyone thought I was too young to remember him. Too young to remember how he was taken from me.

And nobody asked how I felt. Nobody ever asked me if I understood how he died, if I missed him and if I ever wanted to talk about him. Nobody asked, so I thought I wasn't supposed to talk about it. Everyone in this hood knew what happened. There wasn't anything to talk about. He was dead. Killed by a student, a pupil he tried to help. Pops tried to help this community raise themselves up. But even though they became literate, they never lost their ignorance. They considered him one of them. A friend. But a friend on a higher level. They put him on a pedestal when they needed him. But snatched him off his throne when he wouldn't do right by one. Out of hundreds, he couldn't please one. One who took his crown and his life. All I know is, if I fit in and not try to accomplish anything or teach nobody nothing, I won't get a pedestal. And I won't get dead. Live amongst the crabs in the barrel and never try to climb out. Because in the end, they won't let you.

Finally he let me go and wipes my tears. "I wanted to get to know you, but not this quick." I laugh. I couldn't help it. He makes things seem better. I feel better. I feel a little safer too.

"C'mon, you hungry?"

I never did eat. Hell yeah I am hungry.

He takes my hand, which startles me. And guides me to the east side of the park. I have never been on this side before. Never knew anything but the west side filled with the dirty playground, the striped basketball court and the littered tennis courts that are used for double-dutch games. I never journey to this side. Was never a need to. But the east side looks cool. He walks me past more trees than I can count. Folks stroll along pebble stone paths with baby carriages and love in their eyes. Water fountains sprout up from a huge lake near the east entrance. The grass is a velvety layer of green cascading over small hills that children of every race rolled down for childhood fun. I have never seen this side. Why? Never looked past da court. Nothing separated this side from my more familiar spot. But then again I never looked in this direction. Xavier has opened my eyes, and my heart.

In the diner, we sit quietly waiting for our food. He looks at me like he's known me all of my 15 years. Like he wants to know more. He takes my hand and holds it across the table.

"You know I was only kidding when I called you my Puerto Rican princess. I know you're white."

"I didn't pay it any mind," I lie. "Most people take me for Hispanic or mixed. How did you know?"

"I knew it because you had no accent."

"Not all Latinas have accents."

"Not all Latinas get sunburn on their shoulders."

Damn! This brother doesn't miss a beat, does he?

"I saw your burn and the way your tan is coming in and I just knew."

"So why did you say I was Rican?"

"To bother you." He shoots me a smile like the devil in a club on a Saturday night. I return the gesture.

"No, I know a white girl in the projects would have a chip on her shoulders. She would have to. I wanted to get under your skin, find out what makes you tick. And besides, how else was I going to get you to the park if I didn't piss you off a little? I knew you'd come for the fight, if for nothing else."

"I *was* going to tell you about yourself. But that's not the only reason why I came."

"Why else?"

I shrug as the waitress brings us our food. Cheeseburger deluxe for me, BLT for him.

"I guess because I like you."

He smiles and proceeds to eat his food. I follow suit, not realizing how hungry I had been. We share a comfortable silence as we steal glances from each other. Somebody from two booths down plays an old cut on the diner-style jukebox mounted on the wall. The Force MDs know what I'm feeling when they croon "Tender Love."

41

CHAPTER THREE

Monday morning and I can't sleep. I'm thinking about X and the day we had yesterday. After we ate, we walked around looking in the store windows. Discussing the latest styles and the current songs. He held my hand the entire time. This brother is deep. He has goals of becoming an NBA star but to be grounded as a businessman first. He had worked his ass off in high school to get a scholarship. Getting A's and a triple double in most of his games. Now he is starting college. He wants to experience everything higher education can offer. But while staying focused on one true thing: the future. I never met anyone who is so hung up on the future and about "making it." It's something to think about I guess. But I have time.

What I'm also thinking about is when he dropped me back at da court last night, he promised to call me. He promised to think about me every day until the next time he could hop a train down here and see me. I never had a guy, well, I've only had one boyfriend, who didn't care that I was white. My relationship with Lance was short-lived.

Lance had been a 6"1" sophomore I met on the second day of my freshman year, last year. Me and Mel had scheduled our lunch on the same period and were sitting at a table in the cafeteria. New York Septembers were funny. The days could be hotter than July in Louisiana. Or colder than the tip of an iceberg. But that day was weird. The morning was so hot, everybody on the bus was fanning themselves with their new notebooks. A few fellas opened the back windows of the bus and we thanked them for it. But that afternoon got cold quick. By fourth period, everyone stayed inside at lunch and wished they hadn't left their windbreakers at home.

Me and Mel were chillin', when a group of guys started throwing paper at our table. One hit me in the head. So I threw the shit back. But it went over the culprit's head and hit Lance. He walked over and got all up in my face. As a freshman, I had to show that I wasn't afraid. Boy or not, we were 'bout to brawl. Well, I guess he liked my don't-take-no-shit attitude, 'cause he asked me to go with him after two days of talking on the phone. He called me "Mommy" a lot. I knew he thought I was Rican. I was scared to tell him the truth, for fear of ruining my new found popularity. I was "Lance's girl." I wasn't about to give up my status as the rising star on the football team's sweetheart. Shit, me and Mel were invited to all the parties and included in all the cliques. That's rare for freshmen, we knew that! Shit, so I wasn't going to spoil our fun just 'cause he never noticed my Casper skin come December. But New Year's rolled around and the crew got together at my house for a night of partying.

Moms had finally given in to Loretta's invitation to celebrate New Year's at "The Room," a tiny bar two blocks away. Since I had the place to myself, I took advantage. I cooked up a storm. Shrimp cocktail, chicken wings, baked ziti, potato salad, greens, biscuits and a 7-UP cake that would've made you slap your momma! The black and gold decorations Mel got were hittin'. Eric and Charlie hit Crazy Man Watts up for half his champagne stock and the night was about to be on. I wanted everyone to see that Lance's girl could cook her ass off. Everything in place, folks started arriving. Things were straight. Lance was loving the attention he was getting from me and his boys. Just when I thought my world could get no better, some drunk ass went into my mom's room to pass out. Seeing the pictures of my moms and pops, it was then that my secret got out. He came out shouting, "Yo, that bitch is white!" I guess it went around the room. Passed 32 brothers, sisters, and Latinas. Landed on the couch where Lance and I sat kissing to the beat of Keith Sweat's "I Wanna Her." Pookie, Lance's ace boon, whispered something to him in the middle of a kiss. Lance stood up and said, "Shit!" I was like, "What?" "You're white!" Just then, Keith stopped singing. Dick Clark stopped counting down and all eyes were on me. Like they expected me to explain. What's there to explain? Lance said, "I didn't know your ass was white!" "And? Does that shit matter?" Thinking my don't-take-no-shit attitude could redeem me. "Hell yeah! I don't want no white bitch on my arm. I'm keeping it real." "Oh, so now I'm a bitch!" Digging a deeper grave. "You're a bitch if you're white! I can't be having nothing other than a sister or Latina on my arm. I'm pro-black. Too many of us go out like that." "Oh, so you playing yourself 'cause you go out with a white girl from the ghetto. A white girl who can get down on the dance floor and in the kitchen. A white girl who has been to all your games and keeps a better record than you do. And a white girl who has done your fucking homework for the past three months." Somebody in the back near the bathroom said, "Damn!"

"Yo, fuck you! You white bitch. You're just after my black dick!"

We hadn't even talked about sex, let alone *do* it. What was he talking about? I wanted to wait and the softer side of this tough man understood that. He just put up the façade that he was getting his.

"Fuck you!" I screamed back, partially because of embarrassment. He didn't need to be spreading our business like that. "You just mad 'cause you love me. You can't love me knowing I'm white?"

Everybody knew Lance loved me. I sweetened his reputation. I was one of the smartest, toughest bitches in the school. And I was cute! Pookie had even heard Lance say he loved me at Christmas when he gave me a gold bracelet. He couldn't deny we were in love. But I guess matters of the heart didn't run as deep as the color line. Because he snatched his bracelet off my arm and left without so much as a look back. Twenty people left with him.

The next three months he didn't look my way. He started going with this dark sister named Kim. She was the slut of Lehman, but I guess he didn't care. He knew she was black and that's all that mattered to him, I guess. The funny thing is, after the breakup, I kept most of my friends, ex-friends of Lance. They knew he was wrong. And they liked me regardless of color. That proved to me that only your true friends will stick by you. It doesn't matter where you fall on

Mrs. Tameki's spectrum, just that you're real, and chill to be around. From then on, I stopped hiding what I was. If you don't like me being white, then step! If you like me as a person, then cool, we can hang. I also stopped letting someone define me. Le-Le is her own woman. No man was ever going to make my identity for me. I walk in my own shoes, never in anyone's footsteps ever again.

That's why I guess I'm awake thinking of Xavier. He likes me regardless. Or so he seems right now. We'll see what he's really all about. He promised to call me after he got moved into the summer house. It's a dormitory where the athletes and summer school students stay. He gets a break before basketball camp begins, so he'll call me around one.

The phone jars me from my thoughts. 6:30. Mel.

"Hello."

"Hey." She sounds like she is whispering.

"What's up?" I whisper, too.

"Nothing. I had to get up for school."

So she is alive enough to go to summer school. "What happened?"

"Freddie was still here yesterday, so she didn't start in on me until yesterday afternoon. I'm surprised you didn't hear her way up on the fifth floor," she chuckles, nervously.

I usually do hear Ms. Green up here, but I wasn't home to get the low down yesterday.

"I wasn't here."

"Where were you?"

"Long story. So what's your punishment for summer school?"

"A curfew."

"A *who*?"

"Girl, on weekdays, I gotta be in the house by ten. And the weekends by midnight."

"Midnight? That's when the party kicks off on Saturday nights!"

"Shit, I know. But I got to follow it for awhile. My mom got crazy on me."

I wonder if Ms. Green pulled out the frying pan. But I don't ask.

Mel doesn't talk about *what* her momma does, just that she gets "in trouble." I do recall one time last summer when Mel wore pants for a week. It was so hot that week, that the crew took the #61 Bus up to Mount Vernon. We hopped the fence to Wilson Woods public pool and swam all night in the cool water. I guess the residents in the area heard us and called the cops. They picked us up and took us to the station. No one cracked when they asked for information to call our parents. Even if I had, Moms would have been too drunk to know that the phone was ringing. Me and Mel asked to use the bathroom. When we got back to the holding room, Sergeant Porky the Pig was holding Mel's school ID. I guess it fell out of her duffel bag. Figures the ID got found then. The last two months of school she couldn't get lunch in the cafeteria 'cause she couldn't find it. So at three in the morning, Ms. Green's video shoot with Freddie was interrupted by a phone call to come get her daughter and her friends. For seven 90-degree days, my ace boon wore jeans. I think Ms. Green left whelps or something on her legs. To this day there's a scar on her right thigh that miraculously appeared.

"So what time you gonna leave for school?"

"Normal time, 7:15. I get out at two."

"All right, so I'll see you later."

"All right."

I try to go back to sleep but hear clatter in the kitchen. That means Moms is up and making coffee. She drinks so much coffee on Monday mornings. She has to sober up for work the rest of the week. Next she'll be hungry. I guess that's my cue to get up and fix breakfast, 'cause I know she finished that cheese danish I bought her. I get up and go to the bathroom. I ignore the smell of vomit coming from the garbage. Like clockwork, Monday is cleaning day.

While Moms sleeps all morning, I clean. Usually I clean when I come home from school. But during the summer, I have to work around her. Her much-needed rest is never disturbed by my vacuuming and mopping. I rush this morning because it's hot. I want to get out on the stoop by eleven. I didn't want to miss a beat of the hood today. I won't have Mel to shoot the shit with me, but I want to make the best of it. I dust and scrub like a maniac. Like that old cut by Donna Summer, I'm working hard for the money. And by Saturday, my moms will treat me right with my allowance. I start the laundry at nine o'clock. Taking the elevator up and down five floors is grueling in this heat. But it had to be done. I can't wait to shower and sit on the stoop with an ice cream sandwich from the Mr. Softie truck. By eleven, a little off schedule, I'm pressing Moms' last nurse's uniform. The window fan blaring on high, I'm done. I hang the uniform on a hanger and pick up the rest of the bunch. I go in her room where she is sleeping like a baby. I hang the bleached white and starched uniforms in her closet. There, I take in the shrine left in my father's honor. She has never cleaned out his side of the closet. His dresser still has his watch and colognes placed as if he got up this morning and chose his scent of the day. As I look around the room, I could see why that drunken idiot at my party flipped out. There are pictures everywhere. Pops and Moms. Before me, pregnant with me and me as a toddler. Pops' graduation picture. Their wedding picture. It's almost eerie when I think about how she keeps all of his stuff. As if he will come home for dinner and get mad if his possessions have been moved. She won't even let me clean his side of the room, just hers. But I sneak in and dust occasionally. I can't stand a clean house with one dusty room. I don't know how she can live like this. I mean, I miss Pops but damn, he's gone. And we can't bring him back.

Showered and lotioning, I try to decide what to do out on the stoop. I'm lost without Mel. Usually we play the radio, talk about the upcoming school year, gossip with Mrs. Wendell or go somewhere. Either to Bay Plaza shopping center in Co-Op City or into Manhattan. I'm gonna miss my running buddy during the day but I'll have her at night to get into trouble with.

Money in hand, I decide to walk down to the corner store. Well, it's more like a five and dime than a corner store. On the stoop, I speak to Mrs. Wendell.

"I hear your partner-in-crime's got summer school."

"Yeah."

"You're too smart for that. Say, where you going?"

"BJ's."

"Will you get me something?" she says slyly.

"Tsk." I suck my teeth. I want to say no but my good sense tells me to keep my two-faced friend happy.

"Yes, what?"

"Some blue yarn from the fabric section. My niece is due next month and I've got to finish her baby blanket." Mrs. Wendell's niece, Shakiya, is up in the White Plains Rehab Center. She got pregnant one night when she asked her supplier for a hit and didn't have any money. She spent the first four months of her pregnancy getting high. Until she fell out one day in the park. They took her to Mt. Sinai and treated her for an overdose. Miraculously, the baby was not affected, so they sent her to detox for the next four months. Now supposedly she gets let out after she has the baby. And only if they can determine that the baby won't be a crack baby.

"I need a whole ball."

I walk to BJ's, saying hi to my peeps along the way.

In the store, I pick up the new *Right On* and *Black Beat* magazines. They both had new Heavy D and the Boyz posters I needed to add to my collection. Plus a New Edition exclusive interview. I also choose some pretty burgundy nail polish. With my cleaning done, I can pamper myself with a manicure. I remember we are out of garlic powder, glass cleaner, and napkins at home, so I add them to my cart. And I go to find Mrs. Wendell's yarn. To my surprise, look who's standing in the fabric section. Ms. Prissy from the other day. We make eye contact but I don't speak. Shit, folks speak to me!

The yarn section is about half the size of a swimming pool. Mrs. Wendell said she needs a whole ball. But there are hundreds of balls of yarn to choose from. "What the hell?" I say out loud.

"What's the matter?"

"Huh?" I say as Ms. Prissy startles me.

"What's the matter?"

"Oh. I'm supposed to buy a ball of yarn so Mrs. Wendell can

finish her baby blanket."

"Is that the woman who sits in the window of our building?"

"Yeah, nosy ass." I smile as I really look at her for the first time. Ms. Prissy has the eyes of a stuffed teddy bear. Black as coal, but warm and sensitive. You can tell she's on the soft side, getting her feelings hurt at the drop of a dime. Her eyebrows are thick and dark. They remind me of Burt from *Sesame Street*; they even grow in one line just like the puppet's. The new singer Al B. Sure has the same feature. Her hair is in these corny pigtails and her earrings are tiny studs. Her pink sundress make her look eight instead of fifteen.

"If she's making a baby blanket, she would want this type of yarn," she says as she points to an aisle of plush, soft yarn. "It's softer and easier to work with."

"Thanks. I'm Le-Le." I'm a tough bitch, but my parents taught me manners.

"Hi. I'm Vanessa." She even has a prissy name.

"So what's up? Why you in BJ's, Nessa?" I'm already shortening her name like I've known her for two years instead of two minutes.

"I heard they had a sewing section, so I came to get material."

"For what?"

"I'm going to make a few more short sets and a pair of linen pants."

"You sew?"

"Yes. Since I was ten. I made this dress."

Yeah, it looks like it, I think to myself.

"I also want to get another latch hook kit."

"A who?"

"I'll show you." She walks me over to the next aisle. There are four shelves stacked with these kits. A box of yarn, some sort of pattern grid and a latch hook with a wooden handle.

"What do they make?" I ask, curious.

"Whatever you want. Every kit is different. This has a flower pattern. You can make a rug with this bird on it. And this rainbow is nice. I have made several pillows out of them. You should try it."

They do look interesting. All you have to do is put the yarn on the grid where it is sprayed in the same color, and use the latch hook to tie a knot. Once all of the yarn is in place, they make a flower or whatever design it is. I am going to be bored with my girl in school all damn day. Maybe this will keep me busy. I choose the rainbow pattern because the sky background matches the blue in my bedroom.

"When you're done, I can make a pillow out of it for you," she says politely.

"Thank you," I say as we walk to the front of the store to pay for our goods.

At the register, Vanessa comes up two dollars short. She looks like she's ready to ball her eyes out when Tina, the cashier, goes off on her.

"Why you ain't got no more money?" Tina yells in her Hispanic accent. "*Adios mios*. You have to put something back."

Vanessa debates what to put back. I guess she doesn't want to part with anything, so she says, "Can I pay next time I come in? My credit is good."

What is she talking about? I guess in her old neck of the woods, rich people let you walk out the store even if you don't have all the money. They probably figure you are an upstanding resident who will return on your word and pay your balance. Tsk. Not here in the Boogie Down! You were shit out of luck if you couldn't pay for something. Or you stole it. No tabs were run here, it was cash, credit cards or get out.

"Here, Nessa." I pull out my money and give her the two dollars.

"Thank you," she says with an apologetic smile.

"Yeah, *gracias*. I don't need this stress before my break," Tina says as she rings up my stuff.

Me and Nessa walk back home together. I don't ask about her story. But I know she wants to hear mine. They always do.

"So where you from?" I say to break the silence.

"Stamford, Connecticut. My parents just got divorced. My dad remarried and has a new family. He cut back on his alimony and we had to move out of the house. My mother lost her case and we have no money. She never had to work, so she got a job as a secretary. It doesn't pay much. So we had to move here."

Damn! I asked her where she was from, not her life story! And besides, I already knew her low down.

A few steps more and I wait for her to ask. But she never does. She will eventually, I think to myself. But not a word is spoken about my racial background by the time we get back to the building.

I hand Mrs. Wendell her yarn. "Thank ya, baby." All sweet like she hadn't swindled it off of me. Inside the hallway, Nessa asks, "So what are you going to do now?"

"I'm going to bring this stuff upstairs and then come down and sit on the stoop."

"May I join you?"

"I guess. I'll be back in five minutes." I take the elevator to the fifth floor. She has to go to the sixth floor. Hearing snoring from Moms' bedroom, I put down my bags and put away the household supplies I had picked up. I go in my room and grab "the crate." "The crate" is a blue milk crate I swiped from the Food Lion. Mel and I fill it with things we take downstairs on the stoop. I put my latest magazines in there, the radio and some tapes. My manicure supplies and that latch hook kit went in on top. I grab an iced tea out of the fridge. I head for the door when I have an afterthought. I grab a second iced tea for Nessa and the cordless phone, it is almost one and X would be calling soon. Or so he said. I meet the new kid downstairs and turn on the radio. I pop in my new Guy tape. Their new song "Groove Me" is hype. Everyone is playing it at their parties. We open our latch hook sets and Vanessa shows me how to pull the fabric through the grid with the hook. My new found friend and I chill on the stoop, sip iced tea, getting to know each other. Mrs. Wendell just smiles.

CHAPTER FOUR

Ring! Ring!

Ten after one, this has to be X. "Hello," I say sweetly.

"Hey."

"Hey," I reply, smiling to myself. I can't believe he called. And close to on time. Guys are never on time.

"How are you?" he asks in his coarse but gentle voice.

"Fine and you? How did move-in go?"

"Grueling. The dorm's elevator is broken. So the stairs were the only way up. Figures I'm on the third floor. But what made it tougher was that I was thinking about you."

Another thing about white people is they blush. I'm the color of a red kidney bean. My smile, the same shape. I giggle a girlish giggle into the phone. Vanessa pretends not to eavesdrop as she does her latch hook. But I see her ears perk up when I giggle.

"I had a good time yesterday, Le-Le. I hope we can hang out more often."

"I had a good time, too. But how are we going to chill more often? You're in Syracuse."

"Don't worry, I've got it covered. The train ride is only $11 round-trip. My friend Shawn goes home every few weeks, I'll come down with him. I have a few breaks between classes and there are a lot of parties you can come up for."

"Damn! You've thought this through, huh?"

"Oh yes. I like you and I want to get to know you. I think we will be good for each other. If you're willing to give me a chance."

Silence. I wonder if he's smiling on the other end, too.

"Le-Le?"

"Yeah?"

"Will you be my girl?"

"Yeah." I'm starting to like kidney beans.

"Cool. Give me your address. I want to write you and send you something."

So I give it to him. And wonder if I'm dreaming. I just got a boyfriend. And an older guy at that! My girls are going to freak! We talk a few minutes more. I tell him about Mel and her sentence. He says not to worry, it sounds like Nessa is cool people. He gives me his class and practice schedule. He won't have much time during the day to talk. But he promises to call or write before he goes to bed. Xavier makes me promise to take some pictures and send them to him, and he will do the same. There is already a party scheduled in July that he wants me to come up for. Says he wants to show me off. We hang up after he blows me a kiss goodbye. Something wonderful is about to happen.

I sit and smile silently to myself, while I continue to do my latch hooking. To my surprise, Vanessa is staring at me.

"Is that what it feels like to have a boyfriend?" she asks, confirming the glow on my face.

"Why? You've never had one?"

"No. My parents think I'm too young. I did like this guy Steven in my class. But I don't think he liked me. Anyway, I'll never know, I won't be going back to my old school."

Man, she can talk! But it's cool. I like her. Her innocence is a breath of fresh air. Compared to the other girls around here, bragging about men and their first times.

"What school are you going to go to in September?"

"Albert Lehman."

"That's where me and my crew go. I might as well get you acquainted with them this summer."

"Thank you. I'd like that."

This girl is so proper. Ms. Prissy needs a makeover by the fall if she's gong to hang with us. Innocent or not, she needs fashion help, big time.

The afternoon passes quickly to my surprise. By the time Mel walks up to the building, me and Nessa are on our second ice cream sandwich.

"What's up?!" Mel says, talking to me but looking at Nessa.

"What's up, girl. How was summer school?"

"All right, nothing to talk about," she says as she looks at Vanessa again.

"Mel, this is Vanessa."

"Hi!" Vanessa exclaims in her perkiest voice.

"Hey." Mel looks at me with a raised eyebrow. Ignoring her obvious question of, "what's up with the stiff?" I ask, "What we getting into tonight, girl?"

"I don't know. I've got a ton of homework."

"They give you homework in summer school?!"

"Hell yeah, and plenty of it."

"Well, hurry up and go do it so we can hang."

"All right. I'll catch you later."

"Yep." I must have read her mind because...

"Walk me up the stairs?" Mel says pleadingly.

"Nessa, I'll be back. I need to check on my moms too, make sure she's up," I lie. I have to make something up to pass the time, Mel wants to talk.

"So, what's up?" I inquire as we walk into the elevator.

"Girl, I don't think I can take school, yo. It's too much."

"What do you mean? Just do the homework and you'll be straight. It'll be over before you know it."

"I don't know, I just don't know. Anyway, what's up with our new neighbor?"

"Oh she's cool. I met up with her at BJ's and we've been chillin' ever since. She talks too much, but Nessa's straight."

I can tell Mel has her doubts. She gets off on her floor. I go to see if Moms is up.

"Hey," I say to the zombie sitting at the kitchen table. She must have just woken up. At least her eyes are alert.

"Hi. Where you been?"

"On the stoop. You hungry?"

"Yeah, but I don't want anything heavy to eat."

"How long you been up?"

"A half hour."

So she was just going to sit up here until I checked in on her. Probably hungry as hell but too lazy to do anything about it. Tsk. Grown woman...and her child has to wait on her!

I proceed to take out some chicken breast and season them. Moms gets up to take a shower. I put together a quick tossed salad and fired up the grill on the fire escape. As I lay a few pieces of chicken on the fire, I think about what the crew might do tonight. I add two more pieces for Mrs. Wendell, just in case.

Like it's the first and last grilled chicken salad I have ever made, Moms sits before me and ravenously attacks her plate of food. Damn, what did that chicken do to her? After giving Mrs. Wendell my peace offering and telling Nessa when I'd be back, I decide I'm famished too.

On very few occasions do Moms and I have a meal together. It's kind of nice. We don't speak but it reminds me of when I was younger. Mom worked the day shift then and was home when I got home from school. Dinner was ready by the time Pops got home and it was like Thanksgiving every night. Moms used to cook the fatted calf for Pops. He used to praise her every night, even when she made meatloaf. And he hated meatloaf! But he loved her. Sharing a meal with Moms reminded me of how much we lost. I try not to think about it but I miss my pops. Tsk. I miss my mom.

The phone rings as I clean the dishes. Mel.

"What's up. Your mom 'bout to leave?" she asks.

"Yeah in a few, what's up?"

"Nothing, my mother won't be having company tonight, so I have to stick to curfew."

"That's cool." I don't feel like going out anymore. Thinking about Pops got me depressed. 'Course I wouldn't tell Mel that. I wouldn't tell anyone. Except Xavier. A smile creeps upon my face and I remember I never told Mel about it.

"Girl, did I tell you?!…"

Mom leaves just as I'm finishing my story. A nod and a "be good" was her way of saying good bye. Gone are the days of hugs and kisses.

"So do you want to head to da court and chill?" I ask, trying to come up with something to do.

"Yeah, that's cool. What time?" Mel is definitely playing it safe.

"Six. I need a nap. Been up since you called me this morning."

"All right, see you on the stoop."

My kitchen back to normal, I head to my bedroom to catch some Zs. That's when I remember Vanessa. I grab my keys and head to the sixth floor. I think she said it was 603.

Click. Click. Click. Three deadbolts later, I know I have the right apartment as Nessa pokes her head through the slightly opened door.

"Hi!" she exclaims.

"Hey. Can I come in?"

She seems hesitant. What?! Does she think I'm going to rob her? Shit! I loaned *her* money! What do I want from her?

She shuts the door to remove the chain. Walking in, I see a carbon copy of my apartment. The projects are all the same. I heard about this new craze called condos; where all the houses on the block looked the same. But cost an arm and a leg. Well, craze or not, the New York Housing Authority invented and patented the lookalike project. Although boxes are everywhere, a tan couch and chair sit in the living room area. A large quilt drapes the bland furniture and brings life to it. A TV sits on top of an unopened box that reads "TV/VCR STAND ASSEMBLY REQUIRED." Pictures of Vanessa's relatives are hung on the walls, sporadically placed. One wall is dedicated entirely to the life and times of Vanessa Stevens. Funny, all of our family pictures are in my moms' room.

Another revelation interrupted, Nessa asks what do I want.

"I want to know if you want to come with us to da court later?"

"*Da* court?" she asks, as if I had made a mistake.

"Yeah, the basketball court down the block."

"Um, what time? Um, I'll have to ask my mom."

"What? You have to ask your mom to go down the block?"

"Well, to be honest, I'm not even supposed to let anyone in if she's not home."

I presume she sees the anger on my face, as if to say "don't do me any favors." Because she adds quickly, "But you know how it is."

"Why would I know that?"

"We're just being cautious for now. You know, new neighborhood and all."

"No, I wouldn't know...I've always been here."

Awkward silence wedges between us.

I cop an attitude so fierce, I walk out like it is *my* house!

Refreshed after my nap, I'm standing in my closet looking for an outfit. My black shorts and Color-block t-shirt would do for sitting around the court watching Shadow and 'em play ball. The phone rings.

"Hey."

"Hey, Myra, what you up to?"

"Nothing. Just got home from work." Myra is 16 ½ and works at Kentucky Fried Chicken. She usually works all day during the summer and part time during the school year. Last year when Myra's oldest sister and her two-year-old twin daughters returned home after being beaten by her husband, her sister had a nervous breakdown. Mrs. Hernandez's check had to support four people. I guess that didn't include Myra anymore. Myra needed money and a way to get out of a house full of temper tantrums. KFC was the best way. Myra is the most goal-oriented person I know. She was promoted a few times from cashier to closer and now she's learning to keep the books. Come September, she's sure she'll be assistant crew trainer. Her dream in life: To own her own KFC franchise.

"What are you and Mel doing tonight? I'm off the next few days. I need to have some fun."

I fill her in on the events of the past weekend. She is happy about me and X. Mel never said how she felt. But Myra is pissed about missing our night at Shadow's.

"What are you going to do without Mel during the day?"
I tell her about Vanessa. How she's kind of square but seems nice. Tell her she is coming tonight. Well maybe. Myra says she'll meet us later.

Looking cool and feeling "fresh," I step out on the stoop. Surprisingly, Vanessa comes out of the building.

"My mom said I could go. That I need to meet people because she doesn't know how long we will be here."

By 6:25, I was tired of waiting. If I know Mel, she never started her homework. And her mom is not letting her leave the house.

Vanessa marvels at the rest of the block as we walk towards the park.

Myra, in a pair of biking shorts that her two-year-old nieces couldn't wear, is standing at the gate waiting. I love Myra. She has four passions in life: tight clothes, gold jewelry, dancing and entreprenueralship. She's my dance partner when we go to the club. Mel just chills in the back sucking face with Junior. But Myra, tsk. That's my girl when it comes to dancing! Always up on the latest songs and moves. Only time we don't get along is when she talks about the future. I have to get off the phone then. She's too ambitious for me.

"Hey, this is Vanessa."

"Myra," my Puerto Rican friend says as she looks Nessa up and down. I knew I should have told Nessa to borrow an outfit. That polka dot sundress is whack! We head into the park to find the fellas. They're chillin' on the sidelines.

"Hey, y'all." I introduce Vanessa. She gets the same response. A nice hello and looks like, "what the hell does she have on."

Friends and bullshitting go hand in hand. Especially when the boys are around. Eric's sitting here, telling lies about the homecoming game last year. Saying he could've won the game if Paxton had thrown him the ball, he was wide open. But from what we all remember, he was under a pile of brothers from Truman High, nowhere to be found. Charlie comes out of his face and says that I ran from a fight with this girl back in March. Myra comes to my defense.

The truth was the girl walked out to the parking lot so we could brawl (she had been bumping into me all night). But on my way out, Myra started throwing up right on the dance floor. To save my girl some embarrassment, I led her to the bathroom and we left out the back door. I wasn't walking out the front door after Myra had thrown up on herself and me. Fuck that! Juan reminds Charlie that I beat that bitch down two weeks later at the March Madness basketball game. Thank you! Le-Le doesn't run from anybody!

The conversation begins to lighten as I tell my crew about Xavier and what's past da court a few yards away. None of them seem to care that there is a small world we've never ventured into. Since she lives a few blocks away, Myra says she used to walk to the east side of the park with her mom all of the time. She and Vanessa appreciate my discovery.

As darkness falls across da court, we know it's time to take it inside or part for the day. Juan suggests going back to my place. I make up a lie so they wouldn't. Shit! I just cleaned my house today! I am not having them mess it up after only a few hours. We could take this elsewhere. With no other suggestion, we break it up for the night. On the way out of the park, Myra grabs me and says kind of loudly, "Your friend is cool, but she definitely needs new gear."

The night ends with good byes and see yas. Myra drives Juan and Eric home in her bucket. I shouldn't talk, 'cause at least she has a car.

Around 11 o'clock my phone rings while I'm watching a movie. "Hey." Mel.

"What's up? What happened to you? We waited for you."

"We?"

"Me and Nessa waited until 6:25."

"So you went without me?"

"Yeah. Myra met us down there." I fill her in on our evening. I can tell she is mad she didn't go. But she never offered a reason why. Oh well. I've learned with Mel not to press her for answers.

At 3 a.m. I hear Moms come in. At 6:30, Mel calls. I have to tell her I don't need a wake-up call now that it is summer. I'm sorry, but I want to sleep late now that school's out. But she's my girl and I can't do it. I'm done with school but she isn't. Yes, Le-Le does have a heart. But I don't know how long it's going to last.

Hours later, X calls me. He and his friends found out about a 4th of July party going down up there. He is so excited. He clues me in on the details but it breaks my heart to think I may not be able to go. Other than my good grades, my mother expects one more thing from me; attending the annual Independence Day barbecue with her family in Connecticut.

Every year she drags me up there to snobby Stamford and tries to fit in with her relatives. And every year they snub her out because they never accepted her decision to marry Pops and move to the projects. My grandfather hated the idea so much that he refused to attend their wedding. For years, my Aunt Trudy and my grandmother have secretly been keeping Moms informed about family events. Hoping if Moms shows up, Granddad will finally welcome her with open arms.

I tell X the low down. I can tell him so many things, it's scary. He understands and asks me to try to come. He really wants to see me. For the next two hours, my boyfriend and I chat about everything. And about nothing at all. Unfortunately he has to go to practice. He tells me he sent me a letter and to watch for it this week. We say goodbye. Man, I can't wait to talk to him again.

As I flip through the soap operas on TV, a knock sounds at my door.

"Hi." Vanessa, perky as all hell. What, does she take a pill?

"Hey."

"What are you doing today?" she inquires.

"Chillin'." I'm sorry if I seem like I have an attitude towards her, but I'm in chill mode. I just want to watch TV and eat today.

"If you're not doing anything today, can you take me shopping?"

Damn! Myra's got a big mouth!

CHAPTER FIVE

The hazy rays of the sun blankets the Bronx like a blizzard over the Midwest. Funny thing about the five boroughs, if you sit very still in the summer sun, you can hear police sirens, fire trucks, water hydrants and loud music all the way up to Staten Island. And that's exactly what I'm hearing while sitting on this corner with Vanessa. Waiting on a bus headed uptown. After Vanessa knocked at my door this morning, she went into this entire speech about the designer clothes she *used* to have when her parents were together. How her and her mom *used* to shop every week. How she *used* to know the store managers at Lord & Taylor and Macy's. About how she used to be amongst the "in" crowd and be the most stylish teenager in her school. Well, what in the hell happened?! Those sundresses she wears are nowhere near stylish. But I wasn't going to let that be my judge on whether or not we hang. Le-Le was not prejudice, in any form...or fashion. That's why I'm taking her to Bay Plaza in Co-op City. The stores have the freshest gear at the most inexpensive prices.

Our wait isn't long as we board the bus. It isn't Saturday or the first of the month yet, so there are plenty of seats to choose from. Usually you can't get a seat on the weekend or after welfare check day. The folks 'round here hop on the first thing moving towards a shopping area; only to spend their money on clothes, jewelry and appliances. Knowing damn well Jo-Jo needs a haircut, Uncle George needs an operation and Big Mama's at home with no heat or food. Some folks don't know what really matters.

Vanessa and I sit in silence while she marvels at the sites along the way. My mind is filled with Xavier. Thoughts of him are consuming me. I start playing the name game. Teasing myself into believing that one day I'll be Mrs. Lisa Martin. When I get home I'm going to practice writing it on paper. I know! I'll write it in bubble letters and hang the drawing on the wall over my bed.

"I'm hungry, you hungry? Can we eat first?" Vanessa says and startles me out of my trance.

"Yeah, I'm getting hungry. We'll make Burger King the first stop on the list."

"What stores are you taking me to?" she inquisitively asks.

"You'll see. Some of the best places to get a lot of fresh clothes for cheap."

"Cheap clothes? What about the quality?" She frowns her face.

This girl is gonna make me slap her!

"Who cares about quality, as long as you look good!" I state rather harshly.

"Oh," Vanessa whispers, a little taken aback.

I guess what former rich people *used* to do was shop for quality merchandise and worry about the cost later. HA! Does she have a lot to learn about style in the ghetto. Rule number #1 is: Always look good. Ghetto style is unique, and based on one thing, appearance! Everybody here just wants recognition for how they look. I'll be the first to admit it. Don't nobody care about the clothes' longevity. Shit, most people 'round here can't spell longevity!

I ring the bell for the next stop. As the bus comes to a halt, I stand up, signaling Vanessa it's time to get off. Suddenly there is a strange sensation going through me. I feel a wave of nausea coming over me. I manage to walk off the bus without a problem. But once my feet hit the pavement, I feel like the rest of me is going to, too. Vanessa grabs my hand to steady me. A sharp pain pierces my left side. And then I'm fine. Just like that, I'm able to stand upright again.

"Are you all right?" Vanessa asks, puzzled.

"Yeah, I'm fine. I just need to eat something." I play it off as being famished, but I really don't know what the hell that was. Oh well, whatever it was, it's gone now.

We proceed to eat and then shop. I really hadn't noticed, but Vanessa is more developed that I would have thought. Her hips and thighs are those of an 18-year-old. She's actually well proportioned. Most black girls are. But she hides her blossoming curves under those sack-like sundresses. While trying on tank tops and shorts, I ask her why.

"My mother told me that a real lady doesn't have to show what she has." I don't know if I agree, especially if it means I can't make a fashion statement. But it does make sense. I have her try on many colors and styles. But she likes the cute, classy outfits the most. She really looks good in blues and black. Like me. At the checkout counter, I secretly smile at Nessa. We have a lot in common.

We make a day out of shopping. It's so easy to do. We flirt with these guys while eating ice cream cones from Baskin & Robbins. Nessa's a great flirt! We head to the arcade and play a few rounds of Pac-Man and Pole Position. We hit up the accessory store for a few things. Nessa buys two hand bags that go with a few outfits. I pick up some necklaces and costume rings to go with mine.

At one o'clock, I make a pit stop and call my mother.

"You awake?"

"Been awake. Where are you?"

"Shopping."

"Spending my hard-earned money. You need to save that money so one day you can move us out of this neighborhood."

Tsk. How does she know what I have to spend? I only spent $200.00 today. And I still have plenty in my after-high-school fund. And it's *my* hard-earned money.

"What time you coming home?" she barks.

"I don't know," I bark back.

"What about lunch?"

"We ate at Burger King." I want to ask her about that weird pain in my side but think against it.

"I meant lunch for me."

"Did you look in the fridge?"

"Not yet."

"Gotta go, Ma." And the connection is broken. I guess the frustration shows up on my face because Nessa asks, "What's wrong?"

"Nothing. Are we finished?" I reply, distracted.

"I thought you wanted to go to the hat store."

"Oh yeah, then we have to leave."

On the bus going home, I sit quietly looking out the window. At a stoplight, I see some girls playing double-dutch on a side street. It looks like so much fun.

Back at the building, we slowly walk up the steps. The sun had progressively gotten hotter and we are tired out from shopping.

"What all did you buy?" the Hawk asks from her perch in the window.

Nessa answers, "Oh, Mrs. Wendell, we got some fresh outfits and cool accessories. Le-Le is the best to shop with." I take my compliment silently.

"I'm glad to see you're getting along," Mrs. Wendell beams with a smirk. "Mel was looking for you, Le-Le." She turns her attention up the block.

"Thank you," I say wearily.

Nessa and I say see ya later and exchange phone numbers. She's going to call me after she does her chores around the house. She has to get cracking because her mom will be home at six.

When I get upstairs, Moms has left already. My kitchen is in shambles. I guess she cooked something herself. It was a strange occurrence but it happened every once in awhile. Moms left me a note that reads, "Aunt Trudy called. The July 4th party is on next week, rain or shine." Like I care! It is her way of telling me not to forget. Damn! What about X?

Tuesday night and there's nothing on TV. I decide to call Mel.

"Hello?"

"Hey."

"Hey. Where were you when I got home from school?" Mel asks.

"Me and Nessa went shopping."

"Damn, Le-Le! Why you couldn't wait for me?!"

I wanted to say, "Like you had any money to go." I was about to when I think, I wouldn't have any either if I didn't get an allowance. And Nessa wouldn't either if she hadn't cracked open her piggy bank of Christmas money.

"You don't get home from school until two! By the time we made it to Bay Plaza, the stores would have been just about closed!" I must admit, I miss hanging with my girl but summer school is something she has to do. And I can't be waiting around while she does it!

To break the tension, I ask, "How was school today?"

"Awright."

"What you doing now?"

"My homework."

Damn, Mel. You got home at two and you ain't finished yet?" See, that's why her ass is in summer school. I told her it would happen if she didn't stop cutting class with Junior. I mean, I cut too but not as much. And I would call my girl Tracy to get the homework assignment. My work was always done. And my grades are always high. But Mel never followed suit. And when I gave her the assignments we shared, she would only occasionally do them. Now she's paying for it. Missing out on the fun.

"I'm almost done. What are you doing tonight?"

"Right now, watching TV."

"I'm coming up to see your new gear."

"And bring those new kicks Junior got for me."

"Speaking of Junior, he officially asked me to go with him today."

"Really! Oooh girl, now we both have boyfriends," I exclaim.

"Yeah, we need to hook up and go out together."

"When X is down this way. Or the three of us can meet him up at school."

"That would be cool."

Mel and I try on my new clothes for a few hours. She touches up my braids and I do her nails. We sit in my room sipping on my mom's rum and coke, and write bubble letters of X's and Junior's names until almost 11 o'clock. We each draw pictures to hang on our walls.

I tape the blue and white portrait that reads "Lisa + Xavier, 2 Gether, 4 Ever" to the wall above my bed. I can't wait to talk to him again.

Eventually, Mel has to go because she has to get up for school. The rest of the night is mine. I relax on my bed, thinking of X.

* * *

At 8 a.m. Wednesday morning, the phone rings. I thought it was Mel, but it's too late for her.

"Hi sweetheart." X.

"Hi." I blush into the phone. Kidney beans can grow just about anywhere, you know?

My boyfriend and I talk for an hour. He tells me about his coach and what an asshole he is. I tell him that I dated an athlete and knew how they can hate their coach one minute and totally commit to him the next. X doesn't believe it's true. I tell him wait and see. I also inform him that I can't come to the July 4th party with him because of the family picnic. He understands. He suggests me and Mel come the week after, if he doesn't come home with his friend Sean. I share my excitement over the gear I picked while shopping with Nessa yesterday. He says, "Please take some pictures and send them to me. I want to be able to see your beautiful face all the time." I promise I will and then he has to go to practice. He blows me a kiss and we hang up. I wonder if his real kiss is as good as an air-blown one. I hope so.

CHAPTER SIX

A normal morning of dozing back to sleep and breakfast is heightened by Nessa giving me a call. We talk for ages as we do chores around the house. Next stop, the stoop.

The sun, not as hot today, it's a pleasure to not have to wear sunblock. My tan is working already and it is only the first day of July. Mrs. Wendell shouts, "Saw Mel this morning." That reminds me, she hadn't called this morning. Must have been running late. "She got a ride to school with that Junior." Damn! Mrs. Wendell didn't miss a beat.

After Mom's one o'clock feeding, I decide to lay down. My stomach feels really weird. I wonder if it is something I ate. Mom's must have left without a word, because when I get up at 4:15 to use the bathroom, I don't hear her.

"*What the hell!*" I shout to myself as I stare at my panties. Could this be blood? And why is it coming out of me? Shit! What do I do? Call 911? Go to the hospital? What's going on?

I wipe profusely, hoping the bleeding will stop. I pull my panties up. Instinct tells me to go look in my bed. I run down the hall, still feeling like I have to pee. My sheets, to my dismay, have a large spot on them. Frantically, I yank them off and throw them in the laundry bin. I hastily put on a new set and run back to the bathroom. "*What the hell?*" I'm still bleeding. I don't understand. I didn't fall. I'm pretty healthy, I only get an occasional cold. So it can't be a medical condition. What do I do to stop it? I begin to panic. Moms isn't home. There is nobody to take me to the clinic. Then I think of Vanessa. Her mom gets home at six. I can sit on the toilet until six and have her mom take me when she gets home. I pull up my soiled underwear and run to the phone.

"Hello."

"Nessa, I'm sick! Your mom gets home at six, right?" I stutter breathlessly.

"Yeah, what's wrong?" Nessa whispers.

Hesitantly, I tell her I woke up with blood in my underwear. And that I need to get to a clinic before I bleed to death.

Vanessa is silent for a moment and then...a laugh rings out from the other end of the line. A hearty, unkind laugh that I have never heard before. Any other time I would have smiled at her laughter. But today is *not* the day! I am bleeding to death and she's cracking up. I tell her so.

"Girl, you're serious, huh?" She finally controlled herself enough to ask.

"What do you mean, I'm dying!" I shriek. Why is she so calm? I thought we were friends.

"Le-Le, you mean you don't know?"

"Know what? Is there something going around?" I didn't hear about an outbreak on the news. Did I step on one of those needles in the hallway and this is AIDS?

"I'm coming downstairs," she says soothingly.

When Nessa comes inside my apartment, she's carrying a plastic grocery bag.

"Le-Le, calm down. First of all, you're not dying and you're not going to bleed to death. There's no reason to go to the clinic."

"But Vanessa, you don't understand, I'm bleeding and it won't stop!" I am seriously in panic mode and this bitch isn't trying to hear me!

"You got your period."

"My what?"

"Your period. Your period is a monthly cycle in which you bleed for up to seven days. All girls our age get it."

"Why? I didn't do anything bad." I pout.

Vanessa seems very calm and patient. I'm hysterical. I hate not being in control. Le-Le is always in control. But Vanessa seems to have all the answers.

"You don't get your period because you're bad. All girls get it. It's completely natural and it makes you a woman."

"Why did I get it?" I am searching for answers.

"Well, my mother said that when a girl reaches a certain age, once a month, the lining in her thang builds up in preparation to get pregnant. When the girl doesn't get pregnant, the lining breaks down and has to come out of her body. And that's how it comes out."

Confused, I say, "Well, now that I got it, what do I do with it?" I am starting to calm down. I feel better knowing it isn't only me that this is happening to.

"Here," she says, handing me the plastic bag. "Take this into the bathroom. Take a shower and read the directions on the box."

I make a pit stop in my room for a clean set of underwear. In the bathroom, I open the box that reads "Tampons." I've seen these advertised on television but I thought they were for older women with kids.

After my shower, I crack the bathroom door. "I'm not sticking this in my thang!"

"Le-Le, just do what it says."

"But..."

"Le-Le, just do it."

I do what the box says but I don't like it. I have never had sex, so having something in my thang is something to get used to. I put on one of the panty liners that Vanessa had also placed in the bag.

When I emerge from the bathroom, walking awkwardly because I have something up my crotch, Nessa is in the kitchen pouring a glass of water.

"Does your stomach hurt?"

"A little."

"Take this aspirin and sit down." I do as I'm told. Vanessa sits next to me and begins to tell me the dos and don'ts of having a period. I recall some things from Health class, but I skipped Health a lot. It was an easy A.

"Buy a calendar, write down the day it starts and ends, so you can keep a schedule. Never have sex right before your period. Use a condom, or you could get pregnant and a STD. If it lasts longer than seven days, call your doctor. Always wear dark clothing just in case you have an accident."

"Damn!" I interrupt. "When did you get your period?"

"Almost two years ago. Right after I stopped going to ballet and gymnastics."

I envy Vanessa. She seems so much more mature to me now.

"I can't believe your mom never told you. My mom warned me at ten."

"All my mother said was one day I'll become a woman. I didn't know that's what she meant," I confess. "I thought girls just got pregnant if they had sex. I didn't know you have to start your period before you could get pregnant."

"My mom says there are so many lies about a woman's monthly. She said her mom never told her the truth. She had to find out on her own. She vowed that she would tell me everything."

Right now, Vanessa is the wisest 15-year-old I know.

* * *

The next three days I stay in the house. I don't feel comfortable going outside. Hell, how could anyone feel comfortable with this thing in their thang!

Vanessa says it is understandable to feel this way, but that I shouldn't seclude myself. But I refuse to even sit on the stoop. She stays inside with me. We watch the soaps, eat junk food and talk about music. I tell Mel. She's happy for me. She hasn't gotten hers yet but she knows she will soon since I got mine and we are so close. I want to tell my mom. But I don't know how to bring it up.

Wednesday night I waited up for her thinking maybe I can talk to her. But she came in and went straight to bed. Thursday afternoon I ate lunch with her. I sit at the table thinking of ways to say it. Wanting to ask her questions. Wondering if she could tell that I'm different. But we ate in silence. And finally tonight, Friday, I have to say something. I remember how my mom and I were close before Pops died. We shared a mother-daughter bond. I want that back. I need it back now.

When Mel calls to ask me if I want to go out, I refuse. She says Myra called her and the crew is going to see Crazy Man Watts. They were going to hang out at Eric's house. Again, I refuse the offer. Mel seems upset. Saying she wants to hang with me since she hasn't seen me much this week. But I need to talk to Moms. And besides, tomorrow is the July 4th picnic in Connecticut. We are leaving early in the morning, I can't stay out late. Moms has taken tonight and Saturday off. She is ironing a tan, linen pants suit to wear. She only dresses up for this occasion. I sit and watch her press precise creases in her pants.

"You gonna take out those braids?" she's telling me, not asking.

I proceed to undo the braids as she wishes. Everything has to be just so for visiting Connecticut. She wants no reason for Granddad to reject us, again, this year.

"Ma."

"What?" she asks, her attention still on her pants.

A bit intimated, I ask, "At what age did you become a woman?"

Moms stops what she's doing and looks at me. Long and hard.

"You having sex with one of these niggers around here!?" she bellows.

"Damn! No, I'm not having sex at all. And since when did they become 'niggers'?" I scream.

"Then what the hell do you mean 'a woman'?"

"Never mind!" I shout and run into my bedroom. *Slam!* goes the bedroom door behind me. I am furious! I can't contain myself. I start throwing my shit all over the room, wishing it was my mom I was throwing them at. Why can't she talk to me? Is she still angry at the neighborhood? Shit, I lost Pops too. And this ain't even about Pops. It's about me! Has she forgotten about her own daughter? Shit, I'm the only one still alive!

* * *

The morning ride on Metro North is awkward, for a few reasons. It is my first day out of the house since I had gotten "the curse," as Vanessa jokingly called it. I have been dictated to wear a pair of black, lightweight dress pants and a sleeveless shirt. I'm not used to dressing up. I feel like another person in my own skin. And my mother has been staring at me the whole ride. I hope she doesn't think I'm going to talk to her now. The feeling has left me.

* * *

For as long as I can remember, July 4th has been spent in Stamford, CT. When I was younger, Moms would get up before the sun and cook a huge breakfast. Pops' job was to wake me up. My eyes would open to the sun's rays, filtering in through the blinds. I would yawn and stretch, breathing in the masculine aroma of Old Spice. I would smile because I knew it was my daddy, fresh from the shower. He would kiss and tickle me for what seemed like hours. Bathed and clothed, Moms would sit us down in front of waffles, eggs and bacon. An anticipated change from the beloved grits and toast we had before work and school. Because I was young, every year I would ask, "Why are we eating a big breakfast today?" And Moms would patiently reply, "Because we're spending the day in Connecticut with family. And we need a large meal to carry us through to the afternoon picnic." And every year I would jump for joy at the thought of a picnic.

A few years ago, my excitement dwindled as I watched my mother get rejected. I hadn't noticed it before. Right after Pops died, Moms needed to feel the presence of family in her life. She packed bags for the two of us in hopes of being asked to spend the entire weekend under Granddad's roof. The invitation never came. In fact, that year we didn't even stay to lunch. We were received in the same manner that ants are received at a picnic. Two hours later, my mom cried herself to sleep in our Bronx apartment. I've hated going ever since.

Now, as Moms and I stand in the parking lot, a light blue Chrysler approaches. Moms gives me a quick once over and nods. My signal to force a smile. Aunt Trudy, the youngest of my mother's sisters, is of a unique breed. She has the intellectual knowledge of a surgeon and the common sense of a jackass. I've always heard Moms tell Pops it's because she was a "change of life baby." But hey, she married rich. All I know is, she's the only one who acknowledges Moms and I as family. Shit, Christmastime is the only time that matters to me.

Dressed in red, white and blue, Aunt Trudy is darker than my girl Myra. What is it with white people, always wanting to be dark, yet never wanting to be around dark people? She and Mom embrace. They exchange the normal "you look great" and "what have you done with your hair" remarks.

The drive to Aunt Trudy's is painful. How many times must she ask Mom about her job? How many times will she say, "Lydia, you should really move back to Connecticut." Every year, my mom responds, "If my family will have me."

Like clockwork, we hang out at Aunt Trudy's house until it's time to meet the rest of the family at Granddad's house. One thing I like about my aunt is her design style. She collects art pieces from all over the world. I particularly love the African masks that are sporadically mounted on the walls in the den. She says they are from a tribe called the Ibe, noted for their unsurpassed workings in iron and metals. One day when Mel and I have our apartment and become secretaries, I want to decorate using the same African artworks.

Three things happen on the way to Grandad's. First, the afternoon sun heats up. A pleasant welcome after the morning clouds. Aunt Trudy has to make a stop to pick up the specialty cake and makes a wrong turn along the way. We waste 20 minutes trying to get back to the street we passed three times. And my mother's heartbeat becomes progressively louder. Aunt Trudy thinks it's something wrong with the car!

* * *

Granddad's estate is just that. A huge white house built in the perfect center of five acres of land left by my great granddad. The complex is massive. One year, Mom's rejection must have come right after the fireworks. I had been so excited from seeing the explosive display that I almost peed in my pants. I ran to the house without anyone noticing and found a bathroom. I lost my way in the "castle" and I guess Pops spent a half hour checking eight of the ten bathrooms for me. We missed our train and Moms was a nervous wreck.

Always told to be on my best behavior here, meaning no cursing, proper English, and table manners, I force my Connecticut smile once again as Aunt Trudy shouts, "Look who's here!" All I can really think of is X and how I'm missing out on a great party. Tsk. These damn people don't care about us. Look at 'em. All I see on their faces is "Here come the fuckin' ants!"

Outsiders usually sit at the last table. But Aunt Trudy squeezes us in amongst the head honchos: Granddad, Grandmother, Aunt Vivian, Aunt Heather, Uncle Jason and Herb. They all cut their eyes at us. I don't know why everyone is staring, not only do we show up every year, but we're not the weird ones at the table. Herb is my Uncle Jason's boyfriend. Last year my uncle announced he was homosexual and had been living with Herb for a long time. But Granddad accepted them. I guess to him, it is worse to live amongst Negroes than to live with a white fag, who incidently has political connections.

The afternoon drags as we aren't included in any of the conversations. Although I'm angry with my mother, it pains me to see her struggle to get a word in edgewise. Granddad dominates the scene. Even the large oaks that circle the backyard lawn seem to bow at his every word. A tall man with a loud voice, he's an important figure head in the law community of Connecticut. A member of ten boards and a chief officer in his law firm, Granddad has a colossal presence. He looks like Colonel Sanders but reminds me of the giant in Jack in the Beanstalk. Large is size, small in mind. Prejudiced prick! I don't know why I call him Granddad, he's never been more than a pain in the ass to my mother. Shit! Even less to me! I could be dancing with my man right now, instead I'm trying my damndest not to curse somebody out! My mother's cousin Daphne keeps watching my table manners. What, does she not think blacks have etiquette? That's right, I said it. I called myself black. They're all I know, all I love. I rather associate myself with them than these idiots any day. My crew or my family? Hands down I'd choose my crew. My neighborhood accepts me. They don't look at me like Sidney Poitier in *Guess Who's Coming to Dinner*.

I assume the afternoon is over as Colonel Sanders pulls Aunt Trudy inside the house. No doubt, he is yelling at her about bringing us again. No doubt, shit will hit the fan any minute. But something happens. Something of a miracle. While the cake is being served, the Colonel asks my mother what size piece does she want. Taken aback, my moms responds in a childlike voice I have never heard before. Their first words in 17 years! The Colonel has never even kicked my mother out directly to her face. He always asks Aunt Trudy to "not let her guests overstay their welcome." Ain't that some shit! So you know this is an event to go down in history! My mom lights up like a cherry bomb firecracker. And although those were the only words spoken, Moms leaves Connecticut with more hope in her eyes that I ever recall seeing.

* * *

Sunday I awake to two annoying sounds. The phone and loud banging noises. I answer the phone because it's the closest to me. Mel.

"Hey, girl."

"Hey," I respond wearily.

"How was the picnic? Like I need to ask."

"It was all right. My grandfather actually spoke to my mom. It shocked the shit out of everyone."

"Well, that's good. What else happened?"

"Nothing. Same as every year. Everyone stared at us and watched us like we're about to go crazy or something on them."

What do they think, you're going to gank them for their money or something?"

"Probably. Tsk. I don't want nothing those people got. But my mom left happy for once, so I guess that means something. Anyway, what did you do yesterday?" I can almost hear the blood vessels in her cheeks begin to pop as she blushes.

"I hung out with Junior."

"I figured that. What did you do?"

"We went to the mall and then he took me out to dinner."

"Did he pay or swindle some free food out of them?" I laughed out loud. Melinda didn't.

"You know, Junior's not like that. He's into more than just stealing and ripping people off. He's got a good business mind and wants to go to college someday."

"Yeah right, when? He's almost 30 now!"

"He is not, he's only 21. And he has plans. Did you know he writes music?"

"When did he tell you that, while he was kissing your neck or stealing your earrings?" This time I wasn't playing.

"Anyway, what are we getting into today?" she says dryly.

"I have no idea," I reply, hating the way she snubbed me off.

"How about the movies? It's supposed to be hot. The a/c will be nice."

A loud clatter sounds from the kitchen.

"That's straight. Let me call you back in a few minutes."

I spring out of bed and open my room door. My room had been kept cool all night with the fan, but the heat from the rest of the apartment hits me like a brick when I enter the hallway. The surge of sudden heat reminds me of my Easy Bake Oven when I was little. It would take so long to heat up and I was always so anxious. I would wait and wait and it would still be cold. Then all of a sudden, the plastic oven became a miniature inferno, ready to receive my sweet inventions.

My hallway feels like that oven and I a cupcake as I head toward the kitchen. Along the way, I stop in the bathroom to check myself. It was Sunday, the last day of my first period. I could almost feel myself getting back to normal. I couldn't wait for it to be over. And to think, I've got to either get pregnant or turn 45 for this to end. I don't know what's worse!

As I proceed down the hall into the living room, I can feel myself turning golden brown. If someone were to stick a fork in me, I'd be done. The heat thickens as I see its point of origin. Moms is in the kitchen, cooking. Of all days, she chooses a 102-degree New York Sunday to cook a meal. I stand in the doorway with my mouth open. Not knowing what to say, my eyes must be deceiving me because there's a plate of bacon, eggs and toast on the table. And grits are simmering in a saucepan.

"Well, don't just stand there with your mouth open, set the table."

A sober mother from long ago works that kitchen like she had never gone astray. She works it like it's hers again, not mine. I do what I'm told and sit down. She sits across from me and proceeds to fix me a plate. *What the hell?!* I don't remember the last time she didn't think of herself first. When we both are served, she begins to eat. I follow suit and it is as good as I remember. There isn't enough cheese in the eggs and no hot sauce on the table but it had been awhile for her. I forgive her instantly.

"Now what's this about you becoming a woman?"

So that's what this is about. Now she wants to talk. When I needed her, she thought the worst of me. Now she wants to be a mother and talk.

"Now you want to be my fucking mother!" says the evil in me.

"Watch your mouth!"

"Tsk."

"Don't ever cuss at me like that. I'm not one of your friends in the street. No matter what, I'm your mother."

"No, I'm the mother! You haven't done shit since Daddy died!"

I wasn't hungry anymore.

"Lisa…"

"Don't fucking Lisa me. Your asshole father finally speaks to you and now you want to talk to me? Tsk. I don't need to talk to you anymore." I stand up. So does she.

My mother looks me squarely in the eye and says, "Sit down and shut up."

The shrill in her voice runs through me like an ice cream headache. Making me think of when I was little and how all she had to do was look at me and my behavior would change for fear of getting a beating. But just as quickly, the feeling leaves me. I no longer have that respect for her. I push my seat back and retreat to my bedroom. I am going to the movies. To watch someone else's fantasies and run from my reality. I wonder if someone would go to see a matinee about a drunken mother who came back to life. None of my friends would pay to see it.

At the bus stop, I am eerily quiet. Nessa keeps looking at me to make sure I am still alive. Making sure I'm not just a figment of her imagination. I am so still and yet full of rage. How could my mother do that? How could she decide to talk to me after all this time, after all I've done? And only because she's feeling a little better about her family. Didn't I mean more to her?

"Le-Le, you okay?" Nessa's childlike voice opens a small window in my house of rage.

I return an expressionless, "I'm fine."

Mel says, "Le-Le, you can tell me."

"No, I'm okay, really. I wish the boys would hurry up. It's almost time for the bus."

"I think we should just leave without them. You know they wouldn't wait for us," retorts Mel.

"That wouldn't be nice not to wait." Nessa, voicing her opinion.

I notice Mel's face harden as she looks Vanessa square in the eye. She looks like she's ready to beat her down.

"You don't know the fellas like we know them."

I feel like I'm watching a tennis match, because I turn to see what Vanessa's response is. She sits there staring at Melinda. Not giving her the satisfaction of an answer. Mel waits but retaliation never comes. I never noticed the tension between them until now. I wonder where it comes from?

Just then, the boys walk around the corner. "What ups" go around as we wait for the bus. You ever realize that sometimes when you're very still, you notice things you haven't seen before? Like how Shadow stares at Vanessa and teases her. Like how Eric's scar from his gang-banging days in California dances above his eye in the sunlight. He never told us how he got it. Just that his mom moved him and his family out here to get away from that life. I also notice Mel's stone face every time Vanessa laughs. I don't know what's up with her but I'll talk to her later.

My mind and body chills out as we ride the air-conditioned bus to Bay Plaza to catch a movie. Some action flick my boys want to see. I try to perk up but everyone sees that I'm not myself. To be honest, the movie is just a two-hour delay in my own ongoing saga. At least it's cool in the theater. Unlike the inferno I eventually have to go back to.

Guilt tears at me as we approach our building. My words had been true but harsh. Mel tries to get me to talk but I'm not ready to. Nessa just walks behind us, silent.

"How was the movie?" the Hawk asks. Damn, she knows everything.

Vanessa replies, "Very good, thank you."

We all sit down on the stoop. Mel is bugging me to talk. Saying she's my friend and she can help me. That we have been through so much, why can't I tell her what's wrong. My only response is "I don't feel like talking about it right now." But she won't back off. I'm just about to cuss her out, when a car rolls up in front.

The shiny black Mustang spills Eric B & Rakim's lyrical genius out onto the block. All heads turn to see who it is. Some run up to the car and speak to the owner. They are drawn to the bright headlights. I must admit, the fantasy of riding in that black beauty passes through my mind. Mel must have read me, 'cause she turns to me and we high-five each other. Damn! That car is fresh! It has the flyest rims and the stereo is hittin'! Sleek and mysterious, we all wonder who it belongs to. It has to be a star, nobody else is stupid enough to roll through here in a ride like that. They'd be walking home! I'm sure most of the brothers surrounding the vehicle are having the same thoughts. But check themselves when they remember their parole officer or their time spent in juvey hall. But still, others don't care. They can't see past the bright lights.

As if perfectly choreographed, the superstar finally emerges from the car. Shit! It's Junior! Melinda's eyes bug the fuck out! She looks like she's about to faint. Junior poses up against his ride, taking in the fanfare. His eyes are on the stoop, looking at his woman. I must admit, Junior is cute. His square jaw and goatee reminds me of a model in *Ebony* magazine. But I check myself and remember this is lying, stealing, obsessive Junior I am looking at. Too bad Mel didn't read my thoughts right then. She can't see past the lights either.

"You coming or what?" Junior bellows.

Somehow below the scream of the rap music, I hear Mrs. Wendell mumble a coarse, "Hmph!"

Mel looks at me as if to get my approval for her to leave. Why the hell does she need my approval? My glare says exactly that. As well as "remember how he probably got that car." I don't think she hears my thoughts as she sashays down the stairs to her man. They almost matched, him in a vinyl blue and white Nike short suit, she in her navy blue biker shorts. If it wasn't Junior, I would say they make a cute couple. But I am too busy trying to maintain eye contact with Mel. Ms. Green wants her daughter home at midnight. My ace takes a final look back as Junior fires up the engine. I mouth, "Midnight" as she looks down at her Swatch. As the car speeds off like a rocket, I see Mel shrug at me and lean over to kiss her superstar.

Vanessa and I silently ride the elevator upstairs. Before I get off on five, Nessa says, "Whenever you're ready to talk, I'll be here." I say a quick, "I'll talk to you later," and stand in the hallway. My heartbeat hastens as I turn the key in the lock. I don't know what I'm going to say, if I'm going to say anything. Hell, she needs to apologize to me! But I shouldn't have snapped, she is my mother. She had taught me better.

"Lisa, that you?" A voice from the kitchen.

"Yes," I answer shortly.

"Come here," she bellows.

Moms is sitting at the kitchen table. Hasn't left the chair she sat in at breakfast. Food is still on the table too. Only thing added to the picture is Captain Morgan. He must have arrived after I left. His mission: to comfort Moms from the jagged words I cut her with. She isn't drunk, just tipsy. Her words haven't begun to slur but they are heading down that road.

"Sit down." I stood, not wanting to give in.

"I said sit down, young lady!" Moms screams as if she's at the end of her rope. Her tone startles me into my seat.

"Where have you been?" she asks as she pours Coke into her glass of ice and 80 proof.

"The movies." I sit still, stiller than a fly on the wall.

"What did you see?" I am silent.

"I said, what did you see?!" It's a battle of wills, and she's winning. But I can't back down.

"An action movie."

"Was it good?"

"Yes."

"Lisa."

"Yes?"

"When did you start cussing like that?"

"A long time ago." I exhale as the real topic of discussion starts to approach.

"I never noticed before. I taught you better. You shouldn't curse. Stop it."

Force of habit makes me suck my teeth at her. And as fast as the sound comes from my mouth, her hand reaches across the table. She trades my "tsk" for her "smack." Blushing ain't the only time white folks get red. Being smacked fires up the skin just the same. I can't believe she did it! I don't believe she realizes she did it. She sits calmly in her chair. Shit! What is her problem? My face is burning up and she sits there like it's nothing. She hasn't hit me since I was eight. I remember how much I hated it.

I stood up to leave the room. I can't sit here any longer. The view across the table is getting uglier and uglier.

"Where do you think you're going?"

I don't answer. I grab the cordless phone off the wall and walk towards my room.

"When did you stop respecting me?" she screams at the top of her lungs.

I counter very calmly, "When you stopped being my mother," and I slam the door behind me.

Weak from the strength it took not to hit her back, I fall on my bed. My hands shake as I dial his number.

"Hello." And just like that, my words begin to flow at the sound of his smooth voice.

X listens as no one else can. He never interrupts, never asks a question. Just listens. He doesn't say a word until I'm done. And when the storm inside me subsides, he only says, "You need me. I'll be there tomorrow at ten." To calm my anger, he plays our song, "Tender Love," on his boom box. The sweet melody lulls me to sleep before I know it.

Sweet dreams of marriage fill my mind throughout the night. I dream my mom is at the front of a church, crying tears of joy. She nods her approval as I approach the altar in my gown. X stands alongside my pops, looking devilishly handsome. Pops smiles from ear to ear as he places his hand on X's shoulder. He approves as well. He takes his seat next to Mom and the two seem the happiest I have ever seen. As Xavier takes my hand in marriage, my parents release smiles of jobs well done. Pride for me and their new son-in-law shine through like the unity candle my husband and I light. Heading down the aisle as man and wife, Pops stops X and says, "Take care of my little girl. I can't always be there to protect her. It's your job now and I know you'll do a fine job. Her mother's sorry for the hard times they went through. Alcohol is a dangerous game to play. They almost lost each other, but you changed that. You're a good man, a lot like me."

And just then, it was over. My father's voice disappears into the corner of my mind. I awake missing him. But most of all, I miss my mother.

Monday, July 4th Observed brings many things to the city. Chinese and Italian importers infiltrate the Battery with more fireworks and cherry bombs. Little boys come out from in front of their Atari game systems to shoot the minor explosives in the streets and alleys. A multitude of cops from every borough swarm the island, weeding out the petty criminals. And my man arrives at Penn Station on the 9:54 a.m. train. He buses it uptown to meet me on the stoop. I sit waiting anxiously. Nessa sits with me, wondering if any of the guys on the street is him. I shake my head at every, "Is that him?"

Then my knight appears in crisp white Nikes and denim jean shorts. His white t-shirt is complemented with a plaid green and white shirt that melts with his caramel colored skin. My whole body lights up as I watch him walk down the street towards my building. Vanessa doesn't need to ask. I can feel his anticipation. His eyes tell me he feels mine. I can't contain myself. Part of me wants to keep my cool. Le-Le is always cool. But the other half wants to scream like a six-year-old on a roller coaster. Fuck it! I get on the coaster line and run to my man. He accepts me into his arms and picks me up. He spins me as my pops had done so many times when he got home from work. My heart melts as his naturally and my chemically tanned arms hold each other. I don't want to be away from him this long again. I promise myself that I won't be. I think he makes the same pact because he kisses me like he has never kissed me before. I hear fireworks, but I feel them just the same. When he puts me down, I look up at his six-foot frame. He is beautiful.

"Hey, girl. I didn't know how much I missed you until now." He smiles his angelic smile.

"Me either. I want you to meet my friend."

I walk him up the stairs and introduce him to Vanessa.

"Hi, Vanessa, nice to meet you."

"Nice to meet you too. You can call me Nessa, if you like."

"Thanks."

A very obvious "Ah hem!" resounds to our right. Mrs. Wendell sits waiting for her introduction.

"And this is Mrs. Wendell."

"Good morning, ma'am, nice to meet you."

The Hawk seems to soften into a canary as he speaks with respect for his elders.

"Nice to meet you, too, young man."

We sit down on the stoop. X holds my hand tight.

"How was the train ride down?" I ask.

"Okay, just long. Next time I'll bring my walkman or a book to pass the time."

I just keep staring at him, not believing he's here. And he's here because I needed him.

"So what are you ladies up to today?" he says to Nessa.

She giggles and replies, "Nothing. I better go back upstairs. Call me later, Le."

I nod because I can't take my eyes off of him to bid Vanessa good-bye.

"She seems nice. Where's your friend Melinda?"

The Hawk utters a "hmph" and leaves her perch.

"I don't know. I called her to tell her you were coming down, but she wasn't home," I answer.

"What do you want to do? Talk?"

"I just want to spend time with you."

He blushes and takes my hand. "C'mon, let's take a ride." I would follow him anywhere.

"Where are we going?"

"You ever been to South Street Seaport?"

"No, I've heard it's nice, but I've never been there."

"Good, let's go."

On the train ride down, X keeps his arm around me. Keeping me close and safe. I tell him about this morning. About how when I had awoken this morning, Moms was in the living room on the sofa in a drunken stupor. My kitchen wreaked of the overcooked grits that still laid on the table with eggs and bacon. As always, I cleaned her shit up. I made a tossed salad for her to eat later along with some iced tea and garlic bread. I told him it was like clockwork again around my house.

"Have you tried talking to her again?"

"I don't think I have anything to say to her."

"Yes, you do, Le-Le. You just don't know how to say it."

"She knows what's wrong, she's just too weak-minded to do something about it."

"Maybe she needs your help."

"Tsk."

"Tell her you'd respect her again if she stopped drinking."

"I could care less if she drank." I'm lying and he knows it.

"Le-Le, if she didn't drink as much, she would be the mother she used to be, right?"

"I guess. But I'm the daughter, why do I have to tell her what to do? Shit! I've been the parent too damn long already!"

"I know. Maybe it would help if you told her you still need her."

"Maybe. But right now, I want to talk about you. Tell me about basketball camp. Has your coach gotten better?"

He proceeds to fill me in about his coach and their scrimmage games. He says the party Saturday night was dope and he wished I were there. He admits some heffa tried to get with him. Some chick named Eve, short for Evelyn. Don't let me come up there, I tell him, Eve's ass would be mine!

At the Seaport, we walk through the food eateries and shops. We sample some of the seafood. He tells me he loves shrimp and I promise to cook him dinner sometime soon. He says he wants me in Syracuse soon too. On the pier, we split a lemonade and ask some passersby to take our pictures with a disposable camera we bought. We make a promise that no more than three weeks should pass by without us seeing each other. We stay downtown all day.

Making our way back to Penn Station for the 6:05 train, my man is leaving me!

"I hate this," X says as he hugs me. Our watches say 5:59.

"I do too, but you've got practice tomorrow," I say, trying to convince myself that he has to leave.

"I really enjoyed today. Will you promise me you'll talk to your mom?"

"Yes, I promise." I just didn't promise when.

"Promise you'll talk to her soon." He is getting like Mel, too close to me.

I laugh and promise him I would. We kiss and hug until his train arrives. I am going to miss him, but I am assured by thoughts of seeing him next week. He gently kisses my forehead and gets on the train. I call out to him, "Call me when you get there." And my knight rides his train into the sunset.

The trip back to my house is a quiet one. A revelation sneaks up on me like a cool summer rain. I know I have to keep my promise to X. And I know I have to face Moms sometimes. But I realize that for seven years, I have been the adult. And now I was acting like a child. But don't I have a right to? I revel in my thoughts, trying to answer that question. I designate a plan to speak to Moms. I have so much I need to say, so many things to ask. But not today. Today was my day with X. Today is not the day for anger. Me and anger will talk another day.

I don't think Moms notices when I get back. Her room door is closed and I figure she's sleeping. Drenched with perspiration from being in the sun all day, I go to hop in the shower. Her room door opens just as I'm walking into the bathroom. I'm caught, half-naked. My body and mind are unprepared for confrontation.

"Lisa, I need to say something and I don't want you to interrupt." She stands just inside of her doorway. Her voice clear, her eyes focused on me.

"I know I haven't been right since your father passed. I know you have had to deal with his death on your own, because I couldn't deal with it. And I know that ever since, you have had to take care of me and this house. I'm sorry. I'm sorry that I've let you down. But I'm even more sorry because you don't respect me anymore."

Tears stroll down my mother's face. A pool of regret collects at her chin.

"But don't forget how strong you have had to become from my weakness. Remember that's my strength running through your veins. One day my strength will return. And hopefully your respect for me will too. Until then, I ask for a little time."

My mind is divided. I want to shout, "I've given you seven years" and "Mommy, I love you." All I can do is nod my head. She closes her door. I shower, hoping to wash the anger out of me. Hoping to let forgiveness into my pores.

CHAPTER SEVEN

Tuesday starts with two bangs. First, the thunder and lightning from a summer storm jolts me from my sleep at midnight. Then, as my hood begins to drift back to sleep, another bang sounds into the night. This is no noise made by God. I get up to see if the building is okay. Even though it isn't winter, our hot water heater blows up every once in awhile. Mr. Peters, our super, isn't worth shit!

The phone and sirens ring out into the night.

"Hello."

"Le." It's Mel.

"Someone just got shot in da court, girl! Everyone's on the stoop!" she says in one breath.

I throw on a pair of nylon track pants and a t-shirt. Grab my keys and run out the house. You know Mrs. Wendell is the narrator of the whole story. Apparently, some thugs walked up on another dude, to rob him. Thieves without weapons. But the intended victim was packing! He shot two of them. Two fled on foot, two in a jet-black car.

"Damn," Mel says, "how you gonna be stupid enough to stick up without a weapon?"

"I don't know," I say as a few of the tenants watch the cops and an ambulance speed down the block.

Just then, Ray Ray and 'em come running up the block from da court's direction.

"What up, Ray Ray? What you know?" I yell over the steady fall of rain.

He runs up on the stoop, out of breath. His high-top fade falls

THE OTHER SIDE OF DA COURT

from the rain.

"Yo, all I know is two of them cats is being loaded into the ambulance. And two sped past us in a black Mustang."

"Mustang?" Mel yells in disbelief.

"Yep, but neither of them niggers in the car was Junior." Ray Ray creeps off the stoop to let our minds wander.

"Shit, Le-Le, you think he got shot?" she exclaims. I can't tell if she's crying or getting wet from the rain.

"I don't know, girl."

"Shit, let's go to the hospital."

"Hold on, girl, you can't just roll up in there like that. Pigs will be all over the place."

"Le, I gotta know what happened to him."

"We'll find out tomorrow. We'll go to the hospital if that's where he is."

"Le-Le, I love him, he can't die." Mel sits down on the wet steps.

Mrs. Wendell says a dry "hmph" and the other tenants go back inside.

All night I keep thinking about Mel. I know she must be going crazy. I would be if it was X. But then again, X wouldn't have been caught up in that bullshit. I hope Junior is all right, not for Mel's sake, but for his momma's sake. Nobody should have to watch their child die.

Six thirty. The phone's shrill arouses from a troubled sleep. Mel.

"Girl, it was him. I paged him and he didn't call me back. I need to get to the hospital."

"Mel, you don't know it was him who got shot. Maybe he's just laying low."

"Naw, no matter what, he always calls me back. I have to go."

"All right. I'll find out where he's at from around the way. We'll go when you get back from summer school."

"Shit! I can't go to school, Le-Le! My man is in the hospital and you want me to go learn?!"

"That's what his ass should have been doing instead of sticking people up!"

89

"I thought you were my girl, Le-Le," she says dryly.

"I am, Mel. But I don't think you should forget the things you need to handle. Handle your business and then go to see him. He's not going anywhere!"

"You need to handle being my ace, Lisa. You going or not?"

Damn, I didn't think it was like that. I am only trying to tell her what is right. My friendship depended on me going with her, I know that now.

"Yeah, I'm going," even though I think she should let sleeping dogs lie.

The trek to the hospital is insane. First, we question Mrs. Wendell for some knowledge. We know she knows. After some pleading by Mel, the Hawk proclaims that he's at Mt. Sinai. As we head off of the stoop at 9:30 a.m., Mrs. Wendell yells to Mel, "Fool child, let that man lie in the bed he made." My thoughts exactly.

Junior got messed up pretty bad. He has a black eye and a cut on the forehead. One leg sticks out from under the covers, a blood-stained bandage taped to his right thigh.

"The doctors said I'm going to be fine," Junior professes to Mel the second she stops fussing over him.

"Baby, I thought the worst."

"I know." And he kisses her. "You know your man isn't going to leave you that easily." And the two begin to suck face as I sit in one of the visitor chairs, looking out of the window.

"Thanks for coming to see me," Junior says to me as he lets Melinda up for air.

"No problem," I say, bored with the whole scene.

Mel asks, "Is there anything I can bring you, baby?"

I am getting sick. I head into the hallway for some air. Two cops come walking down the hall and stop at Junior's door. They both look at me and begin to give me the third degree. "Do you know Casey Moore, Jr.?" Casey? "Do you know where he was last night? Before the incident?"

Shit! I check myself because I feel like a thug on Miami Vice. I begin to think I did something! I tell the pigs I just know him from the hood. That's it. Mel walks rapidly out of the room and they give her the same run down.

"Mel, why are you in such a hurry to leave?" I ask when the pigs let us go.

"Because, I just am," she says as we hastily walk out the hospital and out onto the street.

"What did Junior say to you?"

"Nothing." I know she's lying. I know my ace boon better than anyone, and she is lying. That's the look she gives teachers who ask her for her homework. Doesn't she know she can't fool me? She knows something about last night.

We arrive back in our hood around 12:30. The summer sun didn't beat down on us as hard as she has the last few days. In fact, it feels like late spring rather than the heat of summer.

"Well, I'm going upstairs to wake my mother up and make her lunch. What are you gonna do?" I ask a dazed Melinda.

"Nothing, just chill," she says without enthusiasm.

"I think you should call the school and tell them you had an emergency. You should tell them why you didn't show up today."

"Yeah, girl, I'll do that." And she gets off on her floor without a good-bye. She knows something, I know it. And that asshole Junior's name is written all over it.

Surprise, surprise! Moms is up when I come in. And she has made pasta salad for both of us. "Tsk," I say under my breath. How long is this going to last? By late afternoon, our spring sun blossoms into a tropical meltdown. I talk on the phone with Vanessa while being shooed out of every room, because Moms decides to vacuum. She's actually getting on my nerves! But she is trying and I am trying to be nice like X told me to be. But shit! Give it a rest!

Sitting on the fire escape, I hope to defy the vacuum and the heat. I proceed to fill Nessa in on the details of the early morning shooting. Her mom made her stay in the house. From my seat, I have a view of the alley below me, where the building's garbage dumpster sits barren.

I can also see the building to the left of mine. No bigger, no better.

I can see into the windows of at least ten tenants. Particularly into Mr. and Mrs. Baptiste's place. The Jamaican couple who boasts that they have been "happily married" for 32 years. Shit! No wonder they're "happily married." She works days, while he's home with Wanda from down the street. He works nights and she's home with Sylvester. Damn right, they're happy!

My view also has some other perks. Like, I see my ace walk out of the alley! I thought her ass was chillin'! I tell Nessa.

"Where do you think she's going?"

"I have no idea, but I know it's trouble."

"Do you think she'll tell you?"

"Tsk. I don't know, Mel can be stubborn."

"Well, I hope she doesn't get mixed up into anything," Nessa says. Funny, I have a feeling it's too late.

Next day, me and Nessa sit on the stoop, playing cards and jamming to some Eric B & Rakim. You would think our volume was just above a whisper, because this sweet ride pulls up in front with the stereo pumped. What the hell? Mel gets out on the passenger side.

"Who's that?" Nessa leans over to ask me. I was about to say "nobody," when a fine specimen of a black man gets out of the driver's side.

"Aiiiright, Mel. I'll get up withchoo lata." His broken English and West Indian accent only compliments his rough but sweet physique. Golden brown dreadlocks frame his face. He has a body of a runner, slender but toned. I'd drink from his six pack any day! He opens the trunk and hands Mel a cardboard box and something that resembles a key. Rasta Man notices they have an audience.

"What up, cuties?"

Nessa blushes and bats her eyes. I flash him my *Right On* magazine smile and then catch myself. Damn, X.

"Whas your name, beautiiful?" he yells up to me.

"Lisa, Le-Le for short."

Mel tells her fine friend, "That's my ace."

He says, "Well, I hope I'll be seeing more of you," and he flashes me a smile and a wink that made me forget about Xavier. Shit, where was Syracuse? And how the hell do you spell it?

Mel tries to walk right past us. Huh, huh, she's going to give me the down-low on Rasta Man.

"What up, yo, who's that?" I ask, watching his navy blue Buick Skylark roll down the street.

"Nobody. A friend."

"She's holding out on us," Nessa exclaims. Mel shoots her a look that says mind your business. Then she says it.

"Mel," I say, "be cool, damn. We just want to know who the cutie is." I glance at Nessa to see if her feelings are hurt by Mel's quick mouth. Naw, she's cool. She's tougher than I thought. But why the friction between the two?

"His name is Andre."

"Where do you know him from?" I pry.

"Around." She cut her eyes at me. Bitch is lying! I know it.

"Around, just around. Now, I need to go upstairs and do some homework. See y'all."

Before she could completely slip through the door, I say, "Homework? I don't see any books!"

The week passes and I don't see much of my girl. Just the occasional phone call to say what's up. A few times, I knock on her door about dinner time. Ms. Greene never comes to the door. She just yells out, "Who is it?" I know damn well she's in there with Freddie.

"It's Lisa, is Mel home?"

"Naw, she ain't home and she's going to get it when she does get home," is her typical response. Followed by giggling and heavy breathing. Go on, Ms. Greene! Ride your way out of the ghetto! But I can say this, company or not, Ms. Greene makes sure everybody knows when Melinda gets home.

In the midst of trying to track down Mel, I begin noticing changes in Mom. She comes home at night and cleans the kitchen so I don't have to the next morning. Or like on Thursday, she didn't ask me to iron another uniform for her, she did it herself. I don't know what's going on. I guess she's trying to redeem herself. But that shit ain't enough for me to tell her I'm going to see X this weekend in

Syracuse. She hasn't earned that much respect. Not yet.

Since Mel isn't around to help, Nessa assists with my preparations. Mixing and matching outfits, organizing my accessories. Taking Polaroids to leave with my man when I say goodbye.

"Please, girl, you know they're really for the females on campus!" Nessa exclaims. You damn right!

Nessa has a knack for creating looks. She says one day she wants to study fashion and visit Paris. Her mom says she's just wasting time dreaming. Nessa disagrees. She intends to depend on her education, not a man like her mother did. Nessa's mom wanted to be a dancer. When she was younger, her grandmother had taken her on a trip to see the newly organized Alvin Ailey Dance Company of Harlem. An all-black dance troupe who performed various types of movement, ranging from classical ballet to traditional African dance. Mrs. Stevens dreamed of joining. And after years of rigorous training, she almost had a chance. Then she met Jeffrey Stevens, an up and coming surgeon. She could marry and still train, letting him support them. But Mr. Stevens turned out to be a domestic tyrant. Forbidding Nessa's mother from engaging in any activities that didn't correlate with his medical profession, especially dancing.

Nessa vowed she wouldn't let a man stomp on her dreams. She had creativity and could already sew. She is determined to be a designer. I don't know if I agree with Nessa, no man is going to stop me from being me. But as far as dreaming goes, I just want to live.

Friday morning, the day of departure, the phone rings at 6:30 a.m. Mel.

"What's up?"

"Nothing, what's going on?"

"Where you been, Mel?" I ask. Forget the bullshit!

"What you mean? I've been around. I been going to school and hitting the books."

"Tsk. Mel, it's me you're talking to. I thought I was your ace boon."

"Serious, that's where I been."

"Hmph, hmph. You been taking care of Junior, haven't you?"
Silence. Then… "Yeah, how did you know?"
"You haven't been around since that night he got shot."
"How do you know, you've been busy with Ms. Prissy," she says
with a forked tongue.
"What the fuck does that mean? Why are you always lashing out
at her?"
"Cause, Le-Le, I can't stand her."
"You don't even know her. And I'm telling you she's cool."
"Whatever. What are we doing this weekend? I hear there is a
house party Saturday night on White Plains Road. You down?"
"Damn, why didn't you tell me! This is my weekend to go see X
for the first time."
"When did you decide that? You're going without me?"
"Yeah, I'm staying in his dorm room."
"Ooooh girl, talk to me!" And there it is. That gritty, contagious
laugh. I didn't realize how much I missed her.

I fill her in. The plan is to tell Moms I am going with Nessa to her
aunt's house in Pougkepsie for the weekend. Yeah, I know it's a
damn lie, but shit, I could care less. I'm going to see my man and
nobody's stopping me.

I take the three o'clock train to Syracuse. As the train leaves the
city and skyscrapers are replaced by trees, my walkman and
magazines are my only familiar surrounding. Upstate NY looks like
Connecticut. From my window seat, I see signs referencing small
towns. Little suburban villages that look boring as hell. Sort of like
the stories in our English books. There's always a tale about some
town that my colonial ancestors were fighting to keep. About how
the white folks rallied together and elected a leader to drive off the
bad guys, wanting to keep their township pure and simple. Shit! Why
do people always need someone to lead them or to help them make a
better way for themselves? Or to help them do something with their
lives. I don't understand! Le-Le doesn't need anybody telling me
what to do or what to think. I don't need anybody telling me who I am
or how I should be. And I can take care of myself. Why should I make

someone else in charge of my life? And why do people need to rally together? Every man for himself. That way, there's no leaders, no betrayers.

It takes longer than I thought to get here. My train pulls into the station after 6 p.m. While I retrieve my green and blue duffle bag, I look for Xavier. There, at the end of the platform, he stands. Damn, he's fine! Instantly I regret eyeing Rasta Man the other day. No harm in that though, right? But I'd kill X if he did that shit!

He spots me walking towards him. His brown eyes drawing me closer. Finally, he's six-foot frame embraces me and he kisses me like he hasn't kissed me before. He lifts me up as if I were still a child in my Pops' arms. I'm safe again.

"Hey, beautiful," X says as he plants me back on my feet.

"Hey." I blush.

"I've missed you."

"Me too." I didn't want to say too much.

"So what's up? Welcome to my world!" he exclaims. He takes my bag and walks me to the parking lot. His friend Sam is waiting in his new GMC Jimmy jeep. I mean this ride is sweet! Black with silver trim. We are riding in style, music blasting and just chilling. I have a good feeling about this weekend already.

This place is huge! I have never been on a college campus before, but damn, this is nice. X points out the buildings of significance as we pass. The library, the science building, the cafeteria and the student center. I try to envision the campus filled with thousands of students. The only thing I can picture is my high school gymnasium during a party. We had had a spring dance last year that drew in kids from all over. Even my boys Chris and his crew came down from Mount Vernon High School. Yo, there were crazy folks up in there! I wonder if it's like that every day here. X tells Sam to drive past a few of the dormitories. Ain't this some shit! Even college campuses segregate! Like my hood, the black dorms look like projects. And the white dorms are fancy with a courtyard. And they're well guarded. Different city, same shit.

Xavier lives in the athlete's dorm. It's a six-floor complex monitored 24 hours a day by a resident assistant. Apparently that's a nice title for an asshole with the ability to squeal on you if you come in after curfew. A mole with power. But X says on the weekends, the monitor is either this cat Toby or A.J. Both could care less what you did as long as it included food or beer for them. Like I said, different city, same shit.

We go in the back entrance and up to his room on the third floor. Him and Sam are roommates. They have two beds, two desks, and one large walk-in closet. X is so sweet, he has cleared some space on his side of the closet and has given me a clean towel and washcloth.

"So, this is it, Le, just me and you." X smiles and kisses my forehead.

As he places my bag on his bed, I say, "Just me and you? What do you mean?"

"Sam is not staying here this weekend. We have the room to ourselves."

Nervous, I simply say, "Cool." Damn, what am I nervous about? Le-Le doesn't get nervous. I'm acting like I never slept with a guy before. I crash all the time with Shadow and them. We sleep side by side all the time, after a night of creepin'. I'm staying with my man. This fine as hell man over there clearing a drawer for me. Tsk. I'm cool. Le-Le is going to be straight.

"All right, get settled and wash up if you want. I want to take you around campus and show you off. Then I'm taking you out to dinner."

He holds me tightly and gently kisses my lips.

The bathroom next door to X's room is pretty clean except for some guy's toothbrush that remains on one of the sinks. I take a quick shower and wrap X's towel around me. I walk back into the room and he just stares at me. "What?"

"You are so beautiful."

I flash him a smile. But I wonder what he's thinking. Shit! I know what he's thinking! He's got his girl all alone up here butt naked in a towel. I know what the hell he's thinking! Well, he isn't getting this, at least not yet. He might be my knight on a white horse, but he ain't got it like that yet! He can look at me all he wants, my ass is still my ass and he's not getting a whiff of it yet!

"I'll leave so you can get dressed," he says, and closes the door behind him. Damn, I wasn't expecting that.

I have to remember to thank Nessa later. The short white sundress and strappy white sandals she put together for me are blowing X's mind. I feel awkward all dressed up. But he is on cloud nine as he adores my long legs. My tan is working and the white accentuates it. Nessa showed me how to put my hair into a few styles that don't require a ponytail holder. For this occasion, I let my sun-reddened hair hang down my shoulders. And I kissed my lips with a little lip gloss, only because Nessa told me to. X is fine in a pair of cream colored pants, brown silk shirt and brown sandals. He has one of the guys on his floor take two pictures of us, the "cute couple." We walk out into the summer night air, hand in hand.

"We have to stop in the dorm across the way."

"Why?"

"Sam is letting us borrow his jeep."

"Really, why?"

"Because that's my boy. We do stuff for each other all the time."

"So he's your ace."

"Yeah. He's staying in Shelby's room this weekend."

"Shelby's his girl? Is she straight?"

"Yeah, she's cool. Keeps him in line."

A tall chocolate female answers X's knock. She stands statuesque in the doorway with her hands on her hips, like we are bothering her. She is my height with a slim build. Her biker shorts seem to be cutting off the circulation of her muscular thighs. Her arms, pumped from lifting weights. Her hair, dark brown, and her eyes, the same color. They seem to be staring right through me. Shit! If this bitch wants to fight, cool. I'll brawl right here in this dress. Bring it on!

"What's up, X. You must be Lisa. What up, yo."

"Hey, what's up," I say, not to say hello but to cut the bullshit. These damn sandals will come in handy.

"Come in." She opens the door wide enough to let us pass. Her

THE OTHER SIDE OF DA COURT

eyes remain on me the whole time. I stare her down, readying my fists. I wonder what Xavier told her about me. Probably the first thing he said was that I'm white. I bet that's why the bitch is about to step to me. She probably can't stand that a brother is with me. I have read about the problem black women have with interracial relationships involving their black men. During the seventies, there was a surge of black and white couples. Females didn't appreciate them to say the least. Shit, why does it have to be about black and white? Why can't anybody be with whomever they want to be with? Color ain't got shit to do with love! Now this sister wants to jump me because I'm a honkey with a fine brother on my arm. Bitch must be jealous! Or racist, one!

"X, here, man." Sam throws X the keys. "Be good to my baby." Black Power Bitch shoots him a look. "I mean my other baby," and then he smiles.

"Y'all got time to talk? Y'all just gonna jet?" Shelby says.

I just want to leave before I bust her in the grill. But X leads me over to one of the beds and sits me down next to him.

"So Lisa, I've heard so much about you. X talks about you all the time. Tell me about yourself."

"What do you want to know?" I say with some Bronx attitude.

"Just about you. What are you into? What's your plan?"

What is this bitch talking about? I ask her.

"I mean, what do you want out of life, where are you going?"

"Well, right now, we're going to eat, if that's fine by you."

Sam snickers but shuts up after Black Power shoots him a daggered look.

"I meant, what are your goals in life?"

Why is everybody on that shit again? I'm sick of it. Must I have a plan? Can't I just be and just live? Maybe all I want is to survive. But because her man has been so nice, I decide I won't say what I'm thinking.

"Right now, I'm weighing my options."

Xavier stands and says, "We'd better get going."

On the way to the car, I ask, "What the fuck is her problem?"

X kind of smiles and offers, "Don't worry about Shelby. She's just so serious sometimes."

"Tsk," is all I can say. She was about to get a serious beat down. I thought college kids were intellectual and on a higher level. Higher education, I hear, is supposed to make you more worldly and sophisticated. Knowledge is supposed to rid the world of racial intolerance and color lines. I guess Black Power Bitch is the ignorant exception.

Xavier and I head to a fancy Italian restaurant. He is a perfect gentleman and opens every door for me. It's like we're married and are out for a night on the town. As the night goes on, we talk and laugh. I have missed him so much. And he has missed me too.

Afterwards, we come back to his room and change into t-shirts and shorts. A bunch of guys on his floor begin playing spades and drinking down the hall. The dorm monitor is the loudest one of all. X suggests we join the crowd. He introduces me as his girl and the guys say a unanimous "What's up." It's cool to sit and chill with my man. I didn't know he drank, but he's on his second Bud. I didn't want to show out yet, so I milk my first one. X notices, so he leans over and whispers, "Don't be shy, be yourself." That was all I needed to hear. I down the Bud and reach for number two. Then I join in with the usual arguing that happens when spades is being played. Both my man and I play a round and beat the pants off our opponents. He does me proud. His friends are cool too. They seem not to see my complexion, just me. I like them. And I like "college" so far, too.

X and I go to bed around 3 a.m. At first, I don't know what to think about sleeping in the same bed. But I didn't have to worry. My southern gentleman holds me close all night. No migrations to my north or my south. I think I'm falling in love.

Saturday. I awake to kisses on my neck and X playing with my hair. He's been watching me sleep.

"Are you hungry?"

"Yeah."

"Good, let's go to the student center and get bagels. The cafeteria's food on the weekends is disgusting."

We shower and throw on shorts. I wear my denim shorts, a white tank top with a cotton yellow short-sleeve shirt over it. My new blue & white kicks accent the outfit. I show a little stomach, for my man's sake.

Our walk to the student center takes about ten minutes. We walk past classroom buildings and grassy lawns. The campus is overwhelming. It looks nothing like Fordham University in the Bronx, where we have tried to crash many parties. This doesn't even look like New York anymore. More like Connecticut. I imagine Pops walking around a campus like this at his Ivy League school.

Breakfast is followed by a walk in the park. Then we come back and get Sam's jeep to go to the closest mall. They are having a back-to-school sale in a lot of the stores. I see gear up here I know nobody 'round my way will have. I have to get it! I like shopping with Xavier. He goes for cheap and cute just like me. Not that "quality" bullshit Nessa looks for. The cheaper the price, the more you can buy. We come back with bags full of stuff. Our most prized possession are a few Nike sweat suits in blue, gray and orange. We each get a pair of jeans and a few long-sleeve shirts. We also buy matching green ribbed turtlenecks that we promise to wear together one day during the winter.

The plan for Saturday night is to hit this party at a VFW hall down the street. Cool, I feel like partying. But then X says Sam and Shelby are going to go with us. Damn! I don't feel like being bothered with her. But shit, I'm going to have fun regardless of that bitch! I'm with my man!

In the backseat of Sam's jeep, me and Shelby sit. She and the guys are engrossed in a conversation about the brothers who are throwing the party. Apparently they live off campus and this party is a fundraiser for rent. We have those all the time in the Boogie Down. While I sit in silence, I want to stare Black Power Bitch down, but I don't want her to think I'm sweating her. If she wasn't so evil, her ugly acting self might be cute. Actually, she is beautiful. She reminds me of some of the models in *Black Hair* magazine. In fact, she resembles the swimsuit model in this week's *Jet*. I admire her dark features that glisten under the streetlights as we ride by. But pretty or not, my Nikes might have to get scuffed when I kick her ass later. Sometimes it's not good to be pretty and be in a fight. Your opponent knows that and reaches for your face first.

At the party, the music is hittin' and the beer is flowing. They are jamming some Heavy D & the Boyz, "Now That We Found Love," and I have to dance. I step out of my corner while X is off saying hello to someone. I go straight to the floor. I'm dancing so hard, my t-shirt comes off. I expose the sports bra that matches my shorts. Some girl that had been dancing by herself joins me. We have a friendly battle and continue to jam as the DJ mixes in Johnny Kemp's "Just Got Paid." Next thing I know, Shelby's dancing next to me. I stop and look her in the eye. She smiles and says, "Show me what you got, girl." I figure it's a truce and continue to dance next to her.

Exhausted, we sit down with a beer. Shelby takes a few swigs and asks over the music, "How old are you again?"

"Fifteen, why?"

"You're not even supposed to be in here."

"So. What's your point?" I counter, kind of tipsy.

"No point, just letting you know."

I jump out of my seat and yell, "You don't need to let me know anything."

Black Power Bitch stands up, towering over me by a few inches. "You need to settle down, relax, sister."

Shocked by her friendly gesture of calling me "sister," I step backwards. But I still remain poised to fight if necessary. Le-Le doesn't back down from anybody.

"You think I don't like you, huh?" she yells over the music.

"I know you don't."

"Don't assume anything. You don't know me that well."

"And you don't know me to judge me."

"Exactly. That's why I was trying to find out more about you, but you gave me attitude."

"No, you gave me shit the second you saw me."

"You think it was for the obvious, don't you?" she smirks.

"What else?"

"Maybe because me and X go way back. And when he dumped my friend to be with you, I wanted to see what you were about."

Completely taken aback, I chill and sit down. She does too. She leans over and says, "I'm sorry if I was too brash. I care about my boy X. He's one of the more positive brothers up here. He deserves to be with someone who respects that. I thought my friend did, but she just thought he was square because he doesn't do stupid shit like get high."

I feel like apologizing. I shouldn't have assumed Shelby had beef with me. I should have known Xavier only surrounds himself with down-to-earth people. This sister deserves an apology. But instead, I ask, "His ex used to get high?" trying to get her to tell me more about this chick.

Shelby explains over the music, "Yeah, Laurie used to get high. I mean she and I met because we're both on the track team. She's cool people. She just doesn't care about herself sometimes. I introduced her to Xavier when he came to SU, thinking it would do her some good, give her a self-esteem boost. But once X found out that she smoked weed on a regular basis, he stopped seeing her. Then he said he was more interested in some female he met in the Bronx. So as you can see, I was curious about his first pick." Damn, I thought. He never mentioned an ex-girlfriend before. I wonder what she looks like. I bet you she looks busted! Before and after she smokes that weed! I take a sip of beer, wanting to know more about Laurie. But then I think, shit! Laurie is history. I'm his now and there's nothing for me to worry about. Le-Le never worries.

Sam and X saunter over to our table. X's face seems to exude worry that he left me and Shelby alone for too long. I smile to assure him that everything is okay. He smiles in relief.

The rest of the night, we dance as couples. The party is hype. Of course, no matter where black folks migrate or integrate, the damn pigs in blue keep a steady watch. Even in Syracuse where the air is cleaner. Pigs still wreak of prejudice and brutality! They walk in and out of the building all night. And at the end of the party, they plant their hoofs outside in the parking lot, ready, almost coaxing, some action.

Back in X's room, he asks, "So did you have a good time?"

"Of course," I say, "I told you that in the car."

"I know, I just want to make sure. You mean the world to me, Lisa, and I want to show you every emotion you make me feel."

"AAAAHHHHHH!" my mind shouts. This guy is a true gem. But instead of saying that, I only confirm my enjoyment of the night out.

"Good. I am so glad you came up here. I want you to come back every few weeks, okay?"

"Cool. Next time I'll bring some of my crew."

"That's cool. Once classes begin, I'll introduce you to my advisor."

"Your advisor? What's that?"

"An advisor is a teacher within your degree program that you go to for advise on what classes to take. You should meet mine, Mr. Gibbs, he's great."

"Why do I need to meet him? I'm glad he's cool with you, but I don't need to know him." Something inside me is starting to stir. This conversation is bugging me.

"Well, maybe Mr. Gibbs can inspire you to think about your future."

"Shit, X! Is that why you wanted me to come up here? So I can think about my future? There's nothing to think about, I'm going to live. So I don't need you or some fucking queer teacher to tell me what to do with my future!" I shout.

"Le-Le, don't you think you're being stubborn? Open your eyes to a world outside of your neighborhood!" he counters, focusing on maintaining his voice level.

"I have looked beyond my neighborhood. There's nothing but back-stabbers and hypocrites, namely you!"

"I'm a hypocrite now?" His voice began to boom. "Why? Because I see my smart and beautiful girlfriend heading nowhere unless she begins to see the light?"

"What light? What do you want me to see?"

"I want you to see that your plan with Melinda to become secretaries is childish!"

"Fuck you! Who are you to tell me I'm childish!" One similarity between whites and blacks is the crimson glare on our faces when we get angry. "I told you all about me. You knew from the start what Le-Le is about. You can't deal with it? Then step!"

"Fine."

We stare each other down. I can't believe my wonderful weekend is ending up like this. And my relationship with X has gone sour in only a few minutes.

"Fine," I confirm.

I start grabbing my stuff and throwing it in my duffel bag. As I head out his door, he says a solemn, "Where are you going at 4 a.m.?"

Shit! I forgot what time it is. Searching for a smart remark, I stand in his doorway.

"I meant fine, I'll leave you alone about your future." He walks over to me and takes my bag. As he places it on the floor, he never breaks eye contact.

"Le-Le, I feel good about us. And I think you do too. We have our whole lives ahead of us. I just want my future with you to be happy and prosperous. But I can't force you to think about college. You've got to want it for yourself."

"Thank you," I say, humbly. I know he only has my best interest in mind. But it's not necessary. Le-Le can take care of herself, now and in the future.

As I sit on the second to last train heading back to the Bronx on Sunday afternoon, I know I'm going to miss Xavier even more. Damn! Three weeks before I see him again. This is the first time I wish the summer would fly by.

CHAPTER EIGHT

Well, while I was away, the Boogie Down continued to hustle and bustle without me. Monday afternoon, Nessa fills me in on the action that I missed. Mr. Anderson on the second floor got arrested on Friday night because he found out his 18-year-old daughter Camisha is pregnant by Jamal from down the street. I guess Mr. Anderson tried to "impregnate" his foot up Jamal's ass, but his mom called the cops. There was a blackout that same evening. Nessa says it was hotter than hell without the fans. Shadow came over to keep her company on the stoop. She almost got caught by Moms coming out of the building to go to work. But she grabbed Shadow and hid in the alley next to the building.

Wait! The shit gets better! While in the alley, Shadow kissed her! Nessa blushes as she tells me about how they held hands and tongue-kissed. He paused to ask her to be his girlfriend and then kissed her again. Man! You got to be careful of the quiet ones! While they were making out in the alley, Melinda crept out the opposite end onto the next block over. She didn't see them, but they saw her because of her gold jewelry; especially a key that dangled from her link chain.

On Saturday, Nessa had to bribe Mrs. Wendell with a quart of butter pecan ice cream not to tell Moms where I was. I had warned her that would happen. And even though the blackout was over, it seemed like the whole building sat out on the stoop to keep cool. Somebody turned on the radio and it was an instant block party! No wonder the hydrant at the corner is leaking; someone had unplugged it so everyone could enjoy the ghetto waterfall.

"Damn," I say, "I missed all of that?!"

"Uhhuhh," Nessa exclaims. "But I'm sure you have a story to tell me."

As we sit on the stoop, I reveal the details of my trip. Nessa listens attentively but continues to stitch a blue and yellow heart-shaped pillow with her and Shadow's name on it. They make a cute couple. Shadow—smart and affectionate. Nessa—sweet and hopeful. This summer is turning out to be a good one for love. Everyone's getting together. I wish some of us would fall apart. I wonder what Melinda is doing. I miss my girl. Ever since Junior got hurt, she hasn't given me the time of day. If she's going to let him come between us, well fuck her then! I don't need her!

"Damn!" I say again, but this time under my breath. Dejavu is a bitch sometimes, isn't it? Melinda rolls up in the dark blue Skylark just as I'm about to write her off. This time Rasta Man doesn't get out of the car. But he smiles and winks just the same. Before Mel can close the trunk good, he speeds off down the block.

"S'up, y'all?" she says. My ace boon is weighed down by a backpack slung over her left shoulder.

"Hey," I say, sort of happy to see her. And curious...curious to know what she's carrying. "What's up, girl? I haven't seen you in ages. Guess where I was?" The old feeling came back and I wanted to tell my best friend about my trip to see my best guy.

"Le, um...I'll have to call you later. I have tons of homework to do. I'll call you tonight, all right?"

"Bet," I say shortly. She walks past us in a blink of an eye.

Like clockwork, I leave Nessa to go wake up Moms. When I came home last night, she was on her way out to work. She asked me if I had had a nice trip but that's all she had time for. I call her five times until she finally gets up. She drags herself into the shower. I go to the kitchen to begin my routine of preparing lunch. Tossed between a tuna macaroni salad and a grilled chicken salad, I check the pantry to see if we have the tuna or the elbow macaroni. I remember I haven't grocery shopped in weeks. That will be my agenda for tomorrow. For now, I think the three cans of tuna and rigatoni pasta will suffice.

I've cooked enough to know that it helps to clear my mind.

Usually I can come up with the answer to a math problem or study for a test while I'm cooking. I even remembered once that that bitch from 233rd Street still owed Myra money from last summer. All while I'm cooking. Talk about profound encounters. That shit hit me like a ton of bricks! I knew the pantry looked bare. I leave my boiling pot of water and fling open the shutter doors. No Bacardi! No Coke! "What the fuck?" I say to myself. She must have finished all she brought home and was too lazy to get more. Or she drank at Lorretta's this weekend. Yeah, that must be it.

Clean and awake, she comes into the kitchen with her towel wrapped around her. She pours two glasses of red Kool-Aid and sits down at the table, her back to the window. I feel her eyeing me as I fill her bowl with macaroni salad.

"Aren't you going to eat with me?" she says, pleadingly.

"Okay." I remember X and my promise to be nice.

"So, did you have a good time at Nessa's aunt's house?"

"Yeah, it was fun," I respond, enjoying my culinary creation.

"Where does her aunt live again?"

"Upstate New York."

"Where in upstate New York?" she asks intensely. Her stare shoots daggers through me.

"Poughkepsie."

"Oh, okay. Nice country up there, huh?"

"Yeah."

"What did you do all weekend?"

I proceed to lie and tell her that Nessa's aunt took us to an art show and an antique gallery. I make up a story about how she took us shopping one day, to the movies and lunch the next. Moms listens, believing my every word.

"Well, I'm glad you had a great time. Would you go back?" she asks.

"Yes. In fact she invited me back in a few weeks."

"I see. That's nice."

Moms slowly rises and goes to get dressed. Damn! She bought it. I haven't lied this good since I was little. I used to tell Pops that

Mom told me I could have an ice cream cone. Pops would say we were going to take out the trash from dinner. But instead, we would chase down the Good Humor truck and eat melting vanilla and rainbow sprinkled cones on the stoop. Mom was oblivious to our game.

* * *

The rest of the week is uneventful. I grocery shop and hang out with Vanessa every day. The summer really sucks without my ace. By this time during the summer, we would have been to twelve parties, gotten into six fights and would've broken a record of how many times we could visit Old Man Charlie's door for some beer.

It took two weeks, but Mel finally decided to call me.

"Hey, girl, what's up?"

"Hey, stranger, where have you been?" I ask.

"Around. Trying to finish summer school next week."

"Really, it's almost over?"

"Hell yeah and I can't wait."

"What do you think you're coming out with?"

"I don't know but I'm passing, I know that."

"That's cool. So what's up with Junior?"

"He's fine. His leg will be out of the cast at the end of August. And then he promised me he will straighten up."

"What do you mean straighten up?"

"I mean he's going to stay out of trouble and maybe even enroll at City College."

"Really," I say sarcastically, not believing it. She read me.

"Le-Le, don't sound that way. I guess that night in da court really scared him. He wants to stop stealing and get a job."

I know my girl. And she sounds so sure about this. I mean it wasn't her usual talk about her man this and her man that. She may be telling the truth. I guess people can change. Even scheming, stealing Junior. Well, I guess I would change too if someone popped a cap in my leg!

"I'm happy for you and Junior," I say with a little more enthusiasm.

"Thanks."

"Anyway, girl, what are you going to do to celebrate summer school being almost over?"

"I don't know. I haven't been to da court in ages, not since I've been with you." Mel's tone lightened.

"We need to find out where the party is."

"No need girl, my friend André is throwing a barbecue on Saturday."

"André? Rasta Man! Shit! I'm there. Can Nessa come?"

"Why we got to invite Ms. Prissy? I don't think she'll fit in anyway."

"What do you mean? She'll be with us, she'll fit in."

"I'm sorry but I don't like the bitch, Le-Le!" There. It was out. Melinda would hold her tongue no more.

"Shit, Mel! Why you gotta be like that? She hasn't done shit to you."

"I'm sorry. I just don't like her. Can't we just do this ourselves?" she pleads.

"I guess so." How will I tell Nessa? I silently ask myself.

"Cool. The barbecue starts at one. You know we have to wear our freshest gear."

"Yeah." I'm getting excited. "You want to go shopping?" I thought about my allowance and my after-high-school stash. If I manage my money right, I will have enough to give Mel money for her outfit too.

"Naw, I'm straight. I have something to wear."

I know I'm hearing things! "I know Junior didn't steal it with his bad leg, so how did you get the money? You hit Freddie up for it?"

"Um, yeah. Freddie's feeling generous lately."

"Must be all that hot sex he's getting." And there it is. That deep, throaty laugh that I love about my best friend. She's my ace boon again.

I can't contain my excitement over the barbecue at André's. Not only am I finally going to spend time with my girl, but if the other guys at the party are as fine as André, we're going to have a blast! I feel guilty thinking that way but I'm not planning on having a relationship with any of them. I care a lot for Xavier. But a girl can look, can't she?

Speaking of looking, I've been noticing some strange things lately. For example, Moms hasn't had a drink in about three weeks. Her "dating" spell has dried up and I wonder why? And yesterday, she actually wore earrings to work. What's up with that? I couldn't believe it. I thought it was somebody else coming out of her bedroom. Her hair was hanging on her shoulders and her tiny gold hoops captured the color of her medium blonde hair. She almost looked like herself again, except....except for her sunken eyes. Moms' eyes used to light up the room. Everyone begged for time with Lydia because of her radiant eyes and charming persona.

* * *

Saturday. Finally. The day me and my ace can chill out. This will be so much fun. What more can I ask for? The summer, my best friend, cute guys, food and alcohol. It's what me and Mel live for.

I feel guilty as I dress in front of Nessa. She helps me coordinate my outfit even though I told her she can't go. She's real cool, I don't know what the hell is wrong with Mel. I stand in the mirror and ask her how I look.

"Good. Red is your color, Le-Le," she beams.

Clad in a red half shirt and red biking shorts, I proceed to tie a light blue and white checkered shirt around my waist. Nessa says the shirt makes a statement. It would keep me comfortable if the night air becomes chilly. And it covers my butt, meaning I'm showing some skin but leaving a little to suggestion. I don't care what it states! It just looks good with my blue and white Puma sneakers. I must admit, I'm cute.

I leave Nessa, promising to give her the details in the morning, and head down to Mel's apartment. I stop dead in my tracks at the elevator when I hear that familiar sound. The entire block hears it! Ms. Greene. She's on the rampage about something. The screams seem to climb the stairs like my Slinky used to when I was seven. Rushing to my girl's aid, I find Mel stuck between the door and its frame. She and her mom were playing tug of war. Ms. Greene wanted her in and Mel wants out.

Mel manages to get an entire leg out into the hallway. While Ms. Greene rants on about a "flunky" and a "failure," I join the winning team and pull my girl to safety.

"Thanks, girl," Mel says, exhausted. "I'd be stuck in the house if it weren't for you."

"What the hell did you do?"

"I didn't do anything. She just flipped."

"Naw, Mel. Your mother never gets that pissed over nothing. What happened?"

"Nothing, I said. Can we squash this or what?"

"I guess." I know Mel well enough to know she's hiding something. But what? We tell each other everything. Or we used to. We walk in silence until my girl perks up.

"So you like my outfit?" she exclaims.

I eye her down. From top to bottom, she's decked out in green. A green and white bandana holds together her freshly done braids. A green t-shirt is the backdrop for a shiny herringbone choker. Her denim poom-poom shorts give way to green socks and white as rice sneakers. Damn! My girl is laid!

"Yeah, you look good." I'll give her that much. I dismissed the idea of going on about how cute she looks, only because of the smirk she just gave me. Like I am the one *green* with envy. Tsk. She better chill out. Ace or not. I'll knock that smirk off her face in a minute. But what's really eating me alive is where did she get the money? She told me the other day that Freddie has been generous. Shit! If Freddie's been that generous, I need to start having sex! And Ms. Greene's got to show me her technique!

She must have read me and known I was about to ask about the money, when she begins telling me who's going to be at the barbecue. André, some of his boys and their females. Some more crews we know from school and some older kids from college. I think of X. I didn't tell him I was going just in case me and Rasta Man hit it off for the night. Wait a minute, don't get me wrong. I love X! But damn that fine André!

The music and smoke tells us we have arrived after we walk about eight blocks. I am parched and all I want is a beer. Fuck the introductions, give me a Bud! But I chill and let Mel introduce me to some people. We make our rounds from one end of the backyard to the center, where Rasta Man sits at the head of a game of spades.

"Whahappenin, ladiiieeees," Rasta croons, eyeing me.

"What's up?" I flirt, flashing my right-on smile.

"You ungry or tirsty? Go eat," he says, getting back to his game.

You don't have to tell me twice. I scope out the cooler and make my way to the grill line. Mel stays behind for a minute. I watch Rasta hand her a link chain with a key on the end of it. She puts it around her neck and begins walking my way.

The cookout is cool. My ace and I chill just like old times. After about our third beer, Mel starts running to the bathroom. Now, my girl has always had a weak bladder, particularly when she drinks, but this is ridiculous. We can't finish a conversation because she's up and off every five minutes. I must admit, the thirst quenchers are making my kidneys go crazy too. So shortly after Mel's fifth trip inside, I follow her.

The backdoor creaks and bangs shut behind me as I stand in the kitchen. The all-white appliances command awe for all of their beauty. I feel as though I'm in a commercial for Windex because I see my reflection all around me. Snatching a chip from a bowl on the table, I cross the room to look for the bathroom. I see a light on the opposite end of the house and follow it. My gosh! Is this really André's house? The kitchen is spotless and now, the dining room is exceptionally polished. There's not a man around who can take care of a house like this. He *must* live with his momma!

I hope the light I'm following will be my path to salvation. I need relief quick, fast and in a hurry. I venture further into the immaculately kept house. Then…I hear Mel's voice. I almost call out to her until I hear a raspy laugh that's not hers. The deep falsetto of a brotha tells Mel that she means business. I follow their flirtatious comments until only a wall stands between us. Normally Le-Le doesn't eavesdrop, but I want to see if my girl is about to cheat on her man. I am actually excited that she might finally rid herself of Junior.

"Anyone ever told you that you have a pretty smile?" the brotha reveals.

"Yes they have. But you still have to pay," Mel counters. What is she talking about?

"You don't play do ya! Okay, okay, here ya go."

"Thanks. Now I think you should leave."

"No wonder André trusts you. You don't take no shit!" They both laugh.

Footsteps pound towards me as I take a seat on the living room couch, as if I am waiting in line. Well shit, I am! They're standing in the small half bath, the light at the end of my tunnel. A very broad, blue-black brotha emerges from the other side of the wall. Yo, Paul Bunyon is enormous! He pauses, winks at me and keeps stepping.

My ace boon is standing over the sink, counting money.

"Mel?" I hesitate. She hastily turns her back to me and drops her cash and a shoe box in the cabinet below the sink. She locks it with the key that dangles from her new link chain.

"Hey, girl," her voice waivers.

"What's up?" I ask inquisitively.

"Nothing, just using the bathroom," she says out of breath. Oh, this bitch must think I'm stupid! Why is she playing games? But I decide to play along, for the moment.

"Who was that?" I ask, referring to Paul Bunyon.

"Who are you talking about? Damn, Le, I was just using the bathroom. What's up with the fucking questions?"

Okay, she took it there. "Excuse the fuck out of me, Mel! I come in here to use the bathroom. And at first I thought you were flirting with Grape Ape, now I don't know what to think!"

"Mind your business, Le-Le, all right!" she shouts and brushes past me, her right shoulder purposely banging into mine. Heated, I grab her arm and force my friend to face me. Never in a million years would I have believed that Mel and I would come to blows. Is it really like that? Does she not trust me enough to tell me what's going on? Tsk. I love her but damn! She's about to get a beat down.

Several inches taller, I stare into her eyes, waiting for her first move. Both of us breathless, anticipating our next course of action, I'm not about to back down. Le-Le don't take shit from anyone, not even my girl.

"Le, you need to back the fuck up," she warns.

"Naw, I ain't going anywhere until you tell me what's in that cabinet," I counter.

"Nothing you need to know about."

"Tsk. Don't give me that shit. What are you up to?" I demand.

"Laaaddiiieeeessss." Me and Mel jump at the sound of André's voice approaching us.

"Everyting okay?" Mel slaps my hand away and walks toward Rasta Man.

"Everything's cool, Dré." And they leave me behind.

Suddenly, my body jolts out of its shocked state, then my bladder reminds me why I had come in the house. I try opening the cabinet while in the bathroom, but to no avail. Shit! I want to know what Mel is doing. I can't believe she won't tell me. We used to tell each other everything. What is happening to her? What is happening to us? My ace and I can't be falling apart. We've known each other since birth. We learned to walk and talk at the same time. We've always been in the same class. Mel and I were weekend students of Pops. And she sat next to me on the pew when we laid him to rest. How could she ever keep anything from me? We're family. We're blood.

Confident is my walk back outside. I was going to write her off back there, but now she's on my shit list. She better watch her back! She must not remember who she's dealing with. This is my turf! I made her popular. I gave her money and clothes! I molded Mel into the round away girl she is. I don't deserve this. Fuck her! She'll get hers sooner or later.

From my seat near the back door of the house, I watch Mel and André flirt and talk smack over a card game. They would have won a few hands if the game wasn't interrupted each time Mel went to use the "bathroom." She walks by me each time. Not a glance, not a stare. Not even an angry sneer comes out of her. I am suddenly alone. I feel loneliness all around me. I sit alone, although seventy people are in the same backyard. My heart feels distant. Mel and her new found mysteries have completely isolated me. I no longer feel like me. I have no ace, no backup, no friend. A part of me is drifting over a waterfall edge into a sea of fear. Le-Le afraid? Yes, all of a sudden. I have always had my ace to keep me company. But more importantly, I have always had her trust. We have fights on occasion. But suddenly I fear we won't make up. I fear losing my best friend, my soul sister. What would I do if she wasn't in my life? What about our after-high-school plans? Would we still be roommates and become secretaries? Damn, that was our plan for the future. That plan doesn't work without her. I've got to talk to her. She's got to trust me with what's going on. I shouldn't have grabbed her, but she brought it there, so I took it there. Maybe I'll give her time to cool down and then try to talk to…

BUCK! BUCK! BUCK!

Gunshots arouse me from my daze. Who's shooting?! Out of my seat I rise, people all around me start running into the house or out of the yard. I seem to be standing still 'cause everyone else is on a chaotic mission to get out of here. Instinct tells me to be no exception. I look for Mel.

BUCK! BUCK!

Shit, where is she?! I duck in and out behind lawn chairs, searching for her. I find the asshole with the gun in the front yard, yelling at a few Latino guys. He is firing into the air for now, but I know that could change with a quickness. I circle around back to the rear of the house and catch a brief sight of Mel and André. Their words seem rushed yet deliberate. He points towards the back door and heads around front.

BUCK! BUCK!

More gunshots! This time sirens follow. Using picnic tables as cover, I lunge after Mel, who's racing towards the house. I stop her on the steps.

"Mel, we gotta get out of here!" I scream, pulling her arm.

"Let go, Le-Le. I gotta take care of this shit!" she says, one hand on the door handle.

"Girl, you crazy! They're shootin' and the cops 'bout to roll up!" I stare her in the eye. To let her know I mean business.

"Lisa, get off me!" she yells in exasperation and pushes me off of her. She runs inside. My heart tells me to wait for her. But again, instinct tells me to run.

Being from the hood, you always follow your gut. So I run out of the yard. I run around the corner and down the street. I run and don't look back. Fear tells me to keep going. Street smarts urges me to forget what I saw. So if I get caught running, I won't know a damn thing. I clear my mind of the whole scene as I run down two more blocks. I can't picture the gunmen or his victims. I just run. Faster than I ever thought I could go. I run towards a safe place. I run home.

Sweat pools down my face and arms. For late afternoon, the New York sun still beats upon us. She is relentless in her efforts to keep us oppressed. There is no escape, no hiding from her 100-degree wrath. But I run. I have to get home. Gunshots still sing in my mind. I can't shake it. So I run faster, hoping I will leave the memories on the block behind me. I run past shops and delis. People without faces. I run for my life, I have to get home and think things through.

The eight blocks back seem to take forever, but my block is finally in sight. I run with all my might. My heart is pumping so loudly, I can't hear the New York hustle and bustle anymore. I don't hear the curses of my frustrated victims as I bump into them and keep going. In fact, I don't hear myself breathing. Home, just a few more yards. I can see it from here. It's hazy, but I see it in the distance. I can see my building, or is it my building? My hearing gone, my vision is getting cloudy. My block's a blur. But I know I am close, so I push harder. Home. I have to get home. I must get…home….

CHAPTER NINE

Oatmeal and raisins stir my senses. I seem to come to life as the sweet aroma comes closer and closer. It tantalizes me so, that it forces me to lift my head. A plate of freshly baked oatmeal and raisin cookies lay before me in a white china plate. Wiping the sleep from my eyes, I realize the coffee table that the cookies sit on isn't my own. I jolt upright into a seated position. Here I sit on a green and white quilted sofa. Knitted white doilies hang over the back and arms, softening the couch's hardened exterior, brought on over the years. The wood coffee table in front of me matches the two on opposite ends of the couch. And two porcelain lamps with ivory shades complete the set. A few feet away, stands a huge floor model television. Accessorized with a hanger and tin foil. The window to my left faces the front of my block. Through cream colored curtains, I find myself staring at the brownstones across the street.

"You're awake."

Mrs. Wendell approaches me from my right. She emerges from the kitchen. Dusk has fallen across the borough and the light that surrounds her serves as a backdrop to the summer night. She carries a plate and glass, and places it on the table along with the cookies.

"I thought the cookies would do the trick," she says, as she turns on the oscillating fan next to the TV set.

"Do what trick?" I ask hesitantly, watching her sit down. She settles into a large recliner that was not made for a feminine frame. The beige and brown comfort chair is proportioned for a big and burly man. Although, Mrs. Wendell seems to be at home in it.

"Fool child, don't you know what happened?" she begins. She

proceeds after I shake my head. "I was looking out my window when I saw you running down the block just as fast as you could. I thought, is that Lisa? Sure enough you got closer and I could tell it was you. You were gasping for air and your legs started to buckle. You collapsed two buildings up. I ran to get you. I believe it was a sun stroke."

Yes, it's coming back to me now. The barbecue. Mel. The argument. The gunshots. Mel.

"Oh my god, Mel!" I shout out.

Sitting up in her chair, Mrs. Wendell tries to calm me. "Be still, young one. Melinda is all right. I saw her walk up the stoop a few hours ago. My God, what were you running from?" she inquired.

I want to say something. I want to tell my story. But I hold back. This is the Hawk that I'm talking to. The entire neighborhood will know what went down in less than an hour.

"I wasn't running from anything," I say under my breath.

"Hmph," she exclaims and sits back in the chair. "Well, go ahead, eat some food. It'll help to get your strength back," and she closes her eyes to relax.

At first I eye the bologna and cheese sandwich she had set before me. Then it calls me and I begin to enjoy its flavor. As I eat, I study the rest of the room around me. Every wall has a story to tell. Pictures of friends, family and church clubs. But the one constant factor in every picture is a large man with big brown eyes. He sits or stands next to Mrs. Wendell in every photo. Both smile from ear to ear. He is very broad, almost a building compared to the other men he stands beside. He seems to smother Mrs. Wendell with hugs and kisses. Literally smothering her with his larger-than-life arms and hands. I didn't know Mrs. Wendell has a boyfriend. Or could this be her husband? I've never seen her with anyone as long as I have lived. The only time I see her is at her perch in the window. I never knew she had a family, let alone a husband. I guess I never took the time to find out. Mrs. Wendell has always been more of a nuisance than a friend. Always trying to get something for nothing. Food or gossip. But I never knew there was a happy, spirited Mrs. Wendell that's been captured in these pictures. And I definitely can't believe she had a man!

I nibble on the oatmeal cookies while I size my hostess up. I guess she could have a man. She isn't that old. Maybe in her fifties. Her jet black hair remains pinned at the nape of her neck, but a bang cascades over her eyebrows. Her floral house dress fills out with ample breasts and Nubian hips. Everyone always said she was originally from the south. Well, her southern roots have adorned her with a huge backside. I never noticed but Mrs. Wendell is definitely a black woman of gracely beauty. Any man in her day would have fallen in love with her. Especially if she had a butt like that back then! Times haven't changed. Brothas nowadays love big asses and big boobs. I'm sure those "assets" will never depreciate in value! And this man that wrapped her up in his arms must have been a major investor.

Curiosity makes me ask, as I wash my food down with homemade iced tea, "You were married, Mrs. Wendell?" The matronly figure stirs at my question.

"Well," she says as she opens her eyes, "yes, I was. A very long time ago."

"I never knew. Where is he at now?"

"Mr. Wendell passed on some time ago, child."

Taken aback, I softly speak words of apology.

"It's okay, you didn't know."

"I've never seen him, have I? He must have died before I was born," I say, answering my own question.

"No, actually you were a young girl when he died." She began to stir in her seat.

"Really?" Curiously, I proceed, "May I ask how he died?"

Twiddling her thumbs, she looks me in the eye. "Well now." And she takes a moment to collect her thoughts. "My Richard passed away in 1982. He was a wonderful man, strong, loving. Good with his hands."

Yeah, I bet! I think to myself, picturing Mr. and Mrs. Wendell fooling around in the bedroom. I bet Ms. Greene and Freddie would have had some competition!

"He was always building something," she continues. "He built that window seat for me. And that bookcase in the corner. Yes, my Richard was beautiful," she sighs. "He was so friendly and everyone loved him." The widow rocks in her chair, and looks out the window. "But how did he die?" I press.

"He was in construction ever since we came to New York back in the 70s. He was the best man on the job. And the best man for that foreman position. He had so much potential and drive. And he desperately wanted that foreman position. Desperately." She chokes back tears and turns her attention back to me.

"Well now, would you like something else to drink? Another sandwich perhaps? You must still be famished." Her voice raised slightly.

She doesn't think I noticed that she never answered my question. That's okay. I hear older people get that way. I'll find out how he died later on. Maybe I can get her to talk more and she'll accidently reveal what happened.

"Young one, I asked did you want anything else?"

"No. No, thank you."

She stands to collect my dishes and walks them into the kitchen. "You sure you don't want to tell me why you were running for your life?" she pried.

"No." I am feeling like myself again, full of attitude. "Are you sure you don't want to tell me how Mr. Wendell died?"

"Hmph! I think we're both smart enough to know when someone's avoiding a question. We better leave well enough alone. Come on, child. I'll walk you upstairs. I know your mother must be frantic." She walks to her front door, keys in hand.

"Why do you keep calling me 'child'?" I sit glued to the couch. I'm not sure my legs will carry me just yet. They tingle with uneasiness, like pins and needles.

"Because you are just a child." She smiles knowingly.

"No, I am fifteen years old. I am no longer a child. Please stop calling me that," I say in my most proper, grown-up voice.

"Fifteen or forty, you will always be a child to me."

Excuse me! What did she say? I don't care if she carried me to safety or fed me. No one calls Le-Le a child. I tell her so.

She retaliates with, "I have watched you grow since the day you were conceived, young one. Don't sit there and tell me you're not a child. You've got childish ways and wherever you were today proves you make childish decisions."

I stand before I counter, letting her know I am grown. "Listen, I take care of my mother and myself. If that's childish, then you're crazy!"

"Cooking and cleaning doesn't make you grown. Grown people make good choices. Grown people don't get involved in stupid situations."

"That doesn't have shit to do with being grown!" I yell.

"Don't cuss at me, little girl! Let me tell you something about being grown. Grown people don't deal with what's given to them. They accept change and make strides. Remember that while you continue to play little girl games with your life!" And with that, she smooths out her dress with her hands and opens the door.

"Your mother is waiting."

I stand and cautiously walk towards her. I cut my eyes at her once up close and out the door.

"My mother isn't waiting for me. It's Saturday. Date night with Captain Morgan."

Keys jingle as she locks the door. "Another thing grown people do is forgive."

I can't take my eyes off of Mrs. Wendell as we stand in the rickety elevator. She watches the numbers light up, while I try to look her in the eye. Who was she to tell me I'm not grown? Tsk. She doesn't even know me or what I'm about. She doesn't even know my story.

Moms answers Mrs. Wendell's knock just as I pull out my key. Moms stands in the door frame glaring at Mrs. Wendell. Mrs. Wendell holds her ground and stares back. Damn! A pin drop can be heard. Not a word is spoken for what seems to be an eternity. I thought they were friends! Moms always found out when I'm creeping from the Hawk. They should be best friends, all the late nights I've had. But rather, they stand silent. Face to face. Poised with unspoken friction. Moms looks puzzled yet relieved. Mrs. Wendell looks calm and sure.

And finally, Mrs. Wendell speaks, "Don't worry, all is well, my dear. Your daughter is still safe." What does she mean 'still safe'? Safe after the sun stroke? Safe from the gunshots? Moms utters a soft, "Thank you," and opens the door wider for me to come inside. The two still look deep into each other's eyes. As if they have words or secrets they don't want to speak of. I hope Mrs. Wendell didn't tell her I ran home. I don't need twenty questions tonight. But what is it that Moms wants to say? Is she holding her tongue? The staring contest comes to an end as Mrs. Wendell takes a few steps backward. As she gets back on the elevator, she concludes, "Your daughter is still safe, for now."

Confusion floods my mind. Moms calls out to me as I rush to my room. Her shouts are anxious. My steps hasten. I can't listen to the interrogation. Not tonight. Not until I think things out. I lock my door behind me. I stand in the middle of my room. My lungs take a deep breath and I fling myself onto the bed. The familiar setting feels the same. Yet I feel different. Somehow I know things are changing.

An instant replay of the barbecue resounds in my mind. I shutter at the thought of gunshots. That sound does something to the heart. It's suddenness pierces your ear and tells your brain that fear, pain and death are at hand. Now, I have heard the pop of a gun many times. Hell! I live in New York! The Crack War is upon us and everyone finds protection and defense in a gun. I don't understand why I was so shaken. Then I ask myself, have I ever been that close to a gun before? I see them on TV. I hear their harsh echoes in the distance. In fact, I had heard that Maurice Clemens brought one to school one day. Everyone in the cafeteria gawked at its sleek black shape. But I never saw it. Mel and I had lunch the period before. The gossip traveled around school. But I never saw it. Well, now I've seen one. Visions of the assailant standing over his prey makes me shiver. I actually feel sorry for the victims. They must have deserved to be frightened like that. You don't piss people off and not expect to be hunted down. Shit always comes back full circle!

Wanting to leave my memories of the gun behind, my mind drifts to Mel. Mrs. Wendell said she came home some hours after me. How long was I out for? How did Mel get out of that scene unharmed? I should call her. We need to talk. My ace is bugging and I don't know why. But I damn sure am going to find out.

"Hello, Ms. Greene? May I speak to Mel?"

"I have no idea where that little hussy is. I'm done with her!" Ms. Greene shouts into the phone.

I hesitate before asking to leave a message. Then I hear a man's voice in the background. "Ask where she may be." Ms. Greene shouts, "She doesn't know, she asked me!"

Confusion on the other line. The phone sounds as if it's a track baton and the competitor has fumbled. Finally, Freddie gets on the line.

"Who am I speaking with?" he asks in a most rational tone.

"This is Le-Le…I mean Lisa."

"Are you a friend of Melinda's?"

"Yes."

"Well, if you know where Melinda is, please let me know. Her mother has been receiving calls all day about her."

"What kind of calls?" I ask cautiously, not wanting to hear an answer.

"Well, the school called. Melinda hasn't been to summer school. She's failed and is going to get left back." My mouth falls open. Freddie pauses as if seeing my reaction. "Then tonight, we've received several calls from the police, questioning her whereabouts. Do you know where she is?"

"No. No, I don't," I answer honestly.

Another runner fumbles and this time drops the baton. Ms. Greene must have grabbed the phone.

"If you know where she is, tell her don't come back to this house! I'ma whoop her ass good! There won't be nothing left for the police!"

I hang up the phone. Not wanting to hear anymore. Mel wasn't going to school? She failed? She was going to get left back? Shit! I knew it! I had a feeling but I didn't want to believe it. All that time, Mel had lied to me. Told me she had homework. Told me she'd call me after school. I can't believe that bitch! She should have told me. Personally I would have done my time in summer school and that's it. Tsk. Actually my grades would have never gotten to that point. But if they had, I would have completed my sentence as best I could. Damn, Mel! I can't believe my ace went out like that. What's going on?

CHAPTER TEN

The next twenty-four hours are crazy. I want to keep to myself and no one will let me. Vanessa wants the low down. Xavier wants to know why I'm so distant. And the worst culprit: Moms. Every time I come out of my room, she's on me. "What are you up to?" "I heard about a shooting, were you there?" "Were you involved?" "What's the matter with you, Lisa?" "Don't turn away from me!" And on and on. Each question is met with my normal response, a closed bedroom door. How can I answer her questions if I don't know the answers myself? Shit! I don't have the answer to a damn thing! *And* it's my business. She wants to be a part of my life now? I don't think so!

I contemplate my next move. I need to talk to Mel. She is the key to my confusion. Once we talk, everything will be fine. We'll make up a lie about where we were on Saturday and things will be cool again. I can come out of my room and get on with the summer. Come fall, I'll help her with her schoolwork and we'll be able to chill like clockwork. She'll be my ace boon again, not the stranger she has become. But it all starts with me talking to her.

Sunday comes and goes. Monday mid-day seems to drag. I'm beginning to get cabin fever. I have to go outside. But I dread the looks and questions. Moms pounds on the door to say she's leaving for work. What do I care? Finally, some peace from all the questions. She gets in one more before I hear the front door close. The house to myself, I unlock the door to freedom.

Grey skies loom over the city, sitting down for dinner and staying for dessert. The gloomy day fits my mood. So many questions, so little answers. I call my crew. Shadow and Eric haven't seen her.

Charlie says he heard about a shooting but doesn't know the details. Just that the pigs picked up the gunmen and brought in his prey for questioning. But Myra has the complete low down, she lives two blocks over. The police must have arrived right after I left. She says they cuffed the Dominican guy with the gun. Apparently, he just wanted to scare the thugs who knelt before him. One of them was having an affair with his wife. You would think the pigs would have left. But Myra says they checked the house while they were there. Word had it there were drugs on the premises. And the owner of the house was the dealer.

Shit! I think to myself as I hang up from Myra. I was at a crack house?! Tsk. I couldn't have been. Yeah, me and my girl have snuck up into some wild places, but never would we sneak up in a drug pin. That shit is dangerous. We don't even walk barefooted in the hallways of our building! You might catch a leftover needle in the foot! Naw, I don't believe it. I'll find Mel and she'll tell me that wasn't a drug pin we got invited to. She'll tell me that André is not a dealer and he must not have known if drugs were at the barbecue. Find my girl and we'll clear everything up!

Around ten o'clock, I open most of the windows in the apartment. Although it's raining, it is hotter than hell. Just as I begin to air out the kitchen, I see a shadow move in the alley below. I step through the window and stand on the fire escape. Anticipation moves me down a few steps. Then I see the reflection of braids and gold ease closer to the trash dumpster.

"Mel!" I call quietly. "Is that you?"

The shadow steps into the dimming light of a broken exit sign on the building next door. It's my ace. I run down the stairs, almost slipping from the dampness.

"Girl, where you been?" I press.

"Around."

"Well, are you okay? Last time I saw you was on Saturday. After the gunshots…"

"Le-Le, look, I'm fine," she interrupts. "I don't have time to talk." She tries to go by me. But I grab her shirt and stop her.

"Mel! We need to talk. I know we had beef at the barbecue, but you need to tell me what's going on. Everyone's been asking questions. Your mother's been bugging out."

"Fuck my mom. She doesn't care where I've been, she's got Freddie. She doesn't need me!" she blurts out.

"Mel, what are you talking about? She's frantic. The cops have been calling your house and everything."

"Let them call!"

I look at her closer in the light. Mel's pretty chocolate complexion is blemished by a black and blue left eye. Her vision seems to waiver as the small amount of light from the exit sign penetrates the swollen area.

"What happened to your eye? Did your mom do that to you?" No answer. "What happened? Mel, talk to me. You're my ace boon! I can help," I plead.

"I don't need your kind of help," she sneers. I take a step back and eye her.

"What do you mean?"

"I mean you left me there to get caught."

"I tried to get you, but you ran in the house," I beg.

"Shit, Le-Le, you were supposed to help me."

"Help you do what?"

"Help me get rid of the cocaine!"

Shit! I take another step back. I try to steady myself of what is to come. I know an explanation is on the horizon. But I'm not sure I'm ready to hear it.

"What cocaine, Mel?" I proceed with caution.

"Shit, Le-Le. Do I have to break it down?" I nod. I didn't have a clue.

Mel sighs. "When Junior got shot, he told me why him and his boys were in da court that night. They had just robbed a few jewelry stores and stashed the goods at a friend's house. While they were at the friend's house, they found another stash of money in the closet. Their boy said it wasn't his and they should leave it alone. But Junior took it and they left. It was worth more than the jewelry they stole.

That's how I met André. That was his money they stole. And to keep him from killing Junior, he needed his debt paid."

I stare at Mel in disbelief. Rain pours down on both of us. My blonde strands stick to my cheeks as the truth unfolds.

"Junior was hurt. So he asked me to do whatever André asked. Le-Le, I didn't want him to kill Junior. I would have done anything for him. You know that," she continued. "I called André on his pager like Junior told me. I told him I would be paying Junior's debt for him. I met him on 233rd Street and that's how it started."

"That's how what started?" I ask, a little naïve.

"Damn, Le! Don't you get it? André sells drugs. I sell drugs for him, to pay off the money Junior stole!"

"Mel, how could you? Are you done? You can get out of it now, right?"

"Why? Why get out of a good thing? I'm the best runner he's got. He told me so. And I'm a girl. The cops don't usually scope females out. I always make my sale and get out clean. I'm getting a cut now too. My own money, Le! No more mooching off of Freddie."

"But Mel," I whisper, "you can't stay in it. You can't live like this. What if you get caught?"

"I won't. André taught me all the tricks," she boasts.

"But what if your mother finds out?"

"So what? She doesn't want me here anyway. I just came to get some more clothes, then it's back to Dré's."

"You're leaving home? You must be out your mind! You can't leave home. What about me?"

"What about you? You left me to deal by myself."

"I didn't know what you were doing. How could…"

"Shit, you were supposed to stay anyway. You were supposed to be my girl. But I guess you've got a new ace."

"Who?" Then it hits me. Is this about Vanessa? I ask her.

"No, it's not all about Vanessa. But what if it were?"

"Mel, you and me are family. Nessa and I are just friends. I mean, look at where we come from. What about our after-high-school plan? I couldn't have that with Vanessa." I hope she's hearing me.

"That's why I wanted you to hang out with André. He says that I'm so good, he wants another female to run for him. Boost business. Le-Le, we could make so much money. We wouldn't have to be secretaries. We could live large! Come with me and you'll see."

I take two more steps back. My back hits the wall of my building. Here we are. Me and my ace. An alley apart. I'm silent. I just stare at this person I no longer know. Does she really think I have found a new best friend? And does she really think I'm stupid enough to get involved in this shit? She must have read me or maybe my doubts show on my face, because she continues.

"Seriously, Lisa. Come with me. No more school or chores. All we do is make runs in the morning. The rest of the day is ours to chill. All we do is eat, drink and party. Me and you can shop all the time. We'll have money coming out of our asses, Le. André will love you. He loves me. And now, I love him."

"Then how did you get that black eye?" I counter under my breath.

She wipes the rain from her face, unconsciously touching her swollen eye. "Beginners mistake. When the cops came, I flushed all the stuff down the toilet. André told me to. But I wasn't supposed to flush it all, just some." She looks down into a puddle at her feet. She steps in it as though she doesn't want to see her reflection.

"So he hit you for that?" I say with disgust.

"Le-Le, are you coming or not?" Her hopeful mood suddenly changed. "I can't stay out here all night. Real black people get naps from the rain."

Damn! What was that? Is my ace bringing color into this? Shit! I can't believe her. First she wants me to break the law with her and now she done crossed the color line. Bitch must be out her damn mind! That's it! André must have knocked her mind right out of her. If he didn't I will!

"Le-Le, if you're my friend, you will come with me."

"How can you say that to me? We are friends."

"What's it going to be, Lisa?" she pressures. "I don't have all night."

We stare each other down. I want to knock some sense into her. Hell, I want to beat the shit out of her! But mostly, I need to say something. But nothing seems to come out of my mouth. And before I can say anything, she is gone. She races towards the opposite end of the alley and disappears into the stormy night. And just like that, I'm alone again.

* * *

Sleep doesn't come easy. My mind plays back the tape of the barbecue each time I close my eyes. And when I finally begin to fall asleep, a reoccurring dream of my confrontation in the alley disturbs me. I wrestle with anger. How could Mel believe she and I were no longer friends? But was she really my friend? Would a friend ask you to leave home and become a criminal? No matter what we've done, I would never break the law. My parents taught me better than that. Pops would roll over in his grave if I started selling drugs. And Moms would have a breakdown. I couldn't do that to her. Shit! I couldn't do that to me.

I toss and turn, trying my best to stay asleep. My legs still ache from the run. But my heart hurts the most. Mel is crazy to think Vanessa has replaced her. And does she really believe Ms. Greene doesn't want her around? I wish I could contact her, tell her to come home. But if I did, did she want to see? Would she listen to reason? We love her. And we want her home. Somehow, though, I don't think Mel will understand. Something tells me she's past the point of no return.

Morning arrives with a shot of sunlight piercing my blinds. Annoyed, I roll over. Sleep seems to have come only moments ago. A loud noise brings me back to consciousness. It sounds like pots and pans falling out of the cabinet. Moms is up and trying to fix something to eat. Well, she can mess up my kitchen today. I don't care. I desperately try to fall back to sleep. But the noises from up front are too much. What is she doing? Maybe I should check on her. Tsk. Naw, everything's cool. I don't feel like being bothered today.

Today, I'm going to rest and think things through. My mind wanders back to Mel.

BAM!

What the hell is that? I spring out of bed as though it were a cannon. And run down the hall, clad in my pajama short set. Just as I thought, Moms is destroying my kitchen. Looks like she's trying to remember how to make pancakes. I stand in the doorway.

"Oh, so you finally came out of your room?" she says, her back facing me. She cleans the remnants of a pancake that had gotten away from her. "Do you want some pancakes?"

I'm not sure if I'm hungry or not. But the aroma arouses my sleeping stomach. I sit down at the dinette and wait to be served. I'll eat and then go back to sleep, I think, as I watch her successfully flip several pancakes. Silently, we begin to eat. She didn't do too bad, they're as light and fluffy as I remember. My reminiscing is interrupted when Moms begins to probe for answers.

"So why have you been in your room?"

I don't answer, hoping she will take my silence to mean I don't want to be bothered.

"Is there something you want to tell me?"

Again, I continue to eat. Doesn't she get it? I'm not in the mood to talk. And especially to talk to her. Like she would listen anyway.

"Are you upset over something Mrs. Wendell said?"

CLANG!

I slam my fork and knife down on the table. That did it. Why the hell is she trying to get in my business? And what does Mrs. Wendell have to do with Mel? I bolt up from my seat. I don't have to listen to this shit!

"Whatever she told you, I can tell you the truth!" Moms yells in desperation.

I stop dead in my tracks. What is she talking about? The truth about what? Does this have to do with their staring competition? What does she think Mrs. Wendell told me?

"The truth about what?" I ask with caution.

Moms lets out a long sigh. "The truth about your father's death," she whispers.

Shit! I feel like I can't move. My feet are planted on the ground. I want to run. Run from another revelation. No more, my mind can't take it. Why now? Why is it she can tell me now? I need to run, but my feet won't listen to my brain.

"Lisa, I'm sure whatever she told you..."

"She didn't tell me anything!!" I shout, cutting her off. She sat in silence, staring out of the kitchen window. I wait. I wait for her words. I wait for something to come out of her mouth. Now that she brought it up, I want to know...or do I?

"Lisa, maybe this isn't the right time," she whispers.

"Shit, Ma! You started this, now finish it!" I yell in exasperation. Am I certain I want to hear this?

Another long sigh comes from the dazed woman in front of me. Moms looks past me out the window. Her eyes fixed on the fire escape. Or perhaps somewhere off in the distance. I stand, waiting to hear the truth about Pops. Waiting to have all my questions answered.

For what seems like hours, Moms sits motionless. I stand my ground before her, waiting. The silence gives way to the faint thump of a heart. The labored efforts of a lung. And the tightening of two throats. I feel scared and somehow anxious. I don't know why this is all coming out now, but I realize I finally need to know. My mind races like a freshly drawn cartoon. The pages of neighborhood gossip flip rapidly through my mind's eye. All the characters make swift and structured movements. Pictures of everything I have heard about my father's death jumble together. The sketches have faded and everything has become so unclear.

Finally, she speaks. In a quiet and calculated voice, Moms begins to unfold the pages of truth.

"The day your father died was...was...a beautiful summer day." Her focus still out the window and into the distance. "He was at the learning center. He had hand-made diploma certificates to distribute them to the students who had passed." A brief smile crept onto her face.

"I remember it took him four hours the night before to write them. He was such a perfectionist. He was so excited that he had helped a few more people get their GED. Patrick always said that if people take the first step toward personal improvement, that everything else would fall into place. He truly believed that this small accomplishment would help them achieve bigger and better things."

Moms blinks back tears, but they're persistent. The salty drops find their way out of bondage and dance in her eyes. With a long sigh, she continues.

"The day he died, we had planned to go out to dinner. It had been a hectic week for both of us and we needed a break. So...you...and I went to pick him up at the center. When we got there, there seemed to be a lot of commotion coming from the classroom." Mom's speech quickens. "I held your hand as we walked down the hall and opened the door." Moms stops and wipes her falling tears. I breathe, anxiously.

"He had a gun." Mom's hands shake as she places them over her bottom lip. It's no use, her lip quivers anyway. "We all told Richard to put it away. He was upset. He hadn't passed. He had taken the course three times and he hadn't passed. Loretta tried to reason with him, 'Take it again, Richard! I'll tutor you!' she screamed. Patrick stood in disbelief. He didn't know what to do. They were great friends. And he had never seen Richard so weak before. He had never seen him cry.

"The others in the room kept their distance. You...you wouldn't stand behind me like I told you to. I wanted to take you outside. But I couldn't move. All I could do was watch and listen to the bickering, the begging, the pleading." She pauses. "You left my side and ran to the back of the classroom to play with the skeleton. I begged you to come to me. I was too frightened to cross in front of Richard to get to you.

"Your father pleaded with him, I remember, Richard had placed the gun..." She sighs. "He had placed the gun in his own mouth."

The life drains from my legs. I fall back into the chair. My mind races. He wasn't going to kill Pops...he was going to kill himself.

"Richard began reciting something. Something I couldn't hear. Everyone was yelling at him, trying to talk him out of it. I managed to make out 'tell her I loved her with all my soul.' Then..."

Moms blinks and looks me in the eye. Her voice becomes steady. She doesn't falter, her words are deliberate. Calm.

"Your father wrestled Richard to the ground, trying to get the gun away from him. The others screamed and yelled. We thought Patrick had succeeded. But the gun went off."

BUCK!

I jump. My head spins. I blink. I hear the shot in my head.

BUCK!

My mind opens and reveals my father laying in front of a desk. I can't see his face. I ask him to tell me the name of the main artery in the heart. I always forget how to pronounce it. But he doesn't hear me. He's fighting with the adults.

BUCK!

I blink rapidly. Moms is crying heavily. She manages to continue. "Your father was shot in the neck. The struggle was over. I remember I laid your father's head on my lap. His blood soaking my dress. You began walking to the front of the room. We tried to turn you away. But...you just kept screaming, 'Daddy, Daddy.' I...I didn't know who to go to, you or Patrick. I stretched my hands to you but my eyes remained on him. He faded fast. He couldn't speak, but his eyes said he loved us always."

Mom blinks and focuses on me at the other end of the table. I'm crying and didn't realize it. I was there? I had seen him die?

"Richard was a pallbearer. He helped me do everything. He was my guardian angel throughout the entire ordeal."

Anger rushes through my veins. How can she say these glorified words about a piece of shit? I think.

"But guilt is a cruel monster. It must have ate at him. After your father was laid to rest...Richard shot himself to death."

Enraged, I stand. "So Daddy died for nothing?!" I scream. "He died in vain?"

"Lisa, you can't look at it that way," she pleads.

"It's the truth. He had stopped him. He accidently shot himself to save that piece of shit, and for what?!" I bellow.

"Lisa, don't. Don't…"

"Don't what? Don't say it? Don't say that Daddy died for nothing! He died for nothing!"

"Lisa, it has taken me a long time to see that your father did the right thing. He did the honorable thing. I couldn't talk about it with you because I knew you couldn't understand, I didn't understand."

I shout, "But why? Did he only care about his student? Didn't he care about us? You know what…fuck the honorable thing!"

SMACK!

My skin stings from her slap. I didn't see it coming. But I watch her hand leave my cheek in slow motion. My mind fizzles between the past and present. I race to my bedroom. I jump into sneakers and run to the front door.

Moms yells, "Lisa, your father loved us. He loved his students. Richard was his friend. Can't you see that no matter what you think, your father did not die in vain? He died for what he believed in!" I'm not trying to hear this shit. I run out the door. Moms' voice behind me screams, "He would've died for his beliefs anyway!" And then sobs.

I am boiling as I run down the flights of stairs. I can't think straight. Mel. Pops. Too much, too much. I push through the front doors of the building and run down the stoop.

"Fool child, come back!" Mrs. Wendell's voice follows me down the street.

Anger and sweat pour out of me. I race down my block, turn the corner. I don't know where I'm going. I just let my feet take me there.

Next thing I know, I'm in da court. Actually, my legs still carry me, they don't stop there. I lunge past the basketball court and the people hanging out. I run past a double-dutch game and stop. I turn to look back at the girls who jump rope so skillfully. So carefree. I pause, knowing I will never join them. I know the game, but will never get to play again. Then my legs begin to move from under me, without asking me first. Pops. Mel. Gunshots. My thoughts fight to stay in the forefront of my mind. But my mind isn't having it. I feel faint and tell my legs to obey my command, to stop. I need to stop. I need to stop and listen to my thoughts.

Here, under the morning sun, I stand. To my surprise, I had run all the way to the east side of da court. Xavier's flower garden blooms in front of me. Not a soul is around. Just me, my garden and my labored breathing. I take a seat on the bench and feel my deepest emotions swell up inside of me. And when they fall, I fall with them. I cry until it hurts. Until I have nothing left. And then I cry some more. Pops. Mel. Gunshots...Pops. Mel. Memories play tricks on me in between the tears. The day Pops died. The barbecue. The alley.

I try to rationalize what happened to my father. What happened to Mel. And what is happening to me. I sit for hours digging into the past. Trying to answer why. Why did Pops die in vain? He was supposed to live for me and Moms. Why did Mel turn to André instead of to me? And why did I know these things now? All this time. Why now? I reflect for what seems to be hours. And one simple word keeps coming to mind. Choices. It's about choices.

I turn around to see the beauty of the park behind me. The pebble stone paths. The rolling green hills. The trees and lake. I face front to see da court in the distance. Familiar yet far away. I revel at the time spent in da court. But I marvel at the change of scenery of the park. Both feel different, new perhaps.

I rise and walk toward da court. I walk down the street, thinking about choices. I head home. I walk in silence, although my hood speaks to me. I walk up the stoop and stand before Mrs. Wendell. I make the utmost effort to look her in the eye.

"Have you stopped running?" she whispers.

"Yes," I hear myself say.

"Good. Well now, you asked me how my Richard died. Maybe you've grown enough to know."

"I already know," I calmly proclaim. Our eyes meet and speak to each other. Having the same conversation she had with Moms.

"Then you know that your father would have done the same for you, your mother and for anyone else."

"Yes." Tears escape from their prison, down my cheeks.

"Then forgive."

I continue my journey upstairs. I walk the five flights and through my front door. Moms is still at the table. She lifts her head and our eyes meet. I walk over to her and instinct tells me to hug her. And I do. We hug and cry, and release. We release the pain, the hurt and the questioning. I feel the anger seep out of me and smile at the forgiveness that steps in.

CHAPTER ELEVEN

As Vanessa and I sit on the stoop sipping iced tea, a fall wind occasionally grazes our uncovered legs. The end of summer is approaching, but it's still warm enough to wear shorts. We listen to the radio and I take in my hood. Everything is changing. The reconstruction of the brownstones is under way. The workers busy themselves from morning to night, erecting scaffolding and pouring concrete. They smile and wave at us as we watch them work. They appreciate the iced tea that Mrs. Wendell sends over every day.

I think about Pops and Richard. I wonder if Richard would have made foreman if he had gotten his GED. I wonder if Pops would be sitting next to me, watching the changes to the neighborhood take shape. But Moms says I shouldn't let my mind get the best of me. She says accept what happened and the way it happened. Find something good in it and treasure it, she says. Well, at first I couldn't. I mean, what's good about learning the cruel truth about my father's death? And what good is it to know that he died for a purpose, and would have done it a million times over if he could? But then I realized, that's the good in it. I've got mad respect for his devotion, to his cause and to his friend. Not many people in this hood have that quality. Shit, look at Mel. All my girl had to do was finish summer school. But she had no devotion. No commitment and no purpose. I worry about what Mel is doing. No matter what, she'll always be my ace boon. But her path was her choice. And I choose not to follow.

Mrs. Wendell interrupts my thoughts and asks, "Ladies, will you do me a favor and go to BJ's for some thread?"

Nessa and I oblige and begin to descend the stairs. As we walk toward the five and dime, I recollect my thoughts and think of what's to come. Soon there will be a lot of new people on the block. Hopefully they'll be cool. Like Nessa. We're starting school soon. I'll miss Mel, but Nessa should fit right in. But if not I won't take shit from anyone. They'll know who they're fucking...I mean messing with, if they attempt to reject her. They'll have the white girl from the projects to answer to.

Yeah, I still acknowledge my whiteness in a black hood. But I try not to spend so much time classifying myself. It finally dawned on me. That shit never mattered to anyone else but me! X doesn't care, he loves me. Vanessa and my crew, they could care less. I finally realized that I was the one who put my lack of color on a pedestal. I chose to use it as a shield. I was trying to be different, without being different at all. I'm done with that. Le-Le is just Le-Le from now on. No more mention of my color or expectations that someone else will mention it. And if they do, they can step! No need to brawl. I mean, I will go to blows if necessary, if it comes to it. Don't think I've lost my edge. But from now on I choose not to look for a fight. I've got so much more to think about than fighting.

Like Moms going with me to meet X next week. And I'm also going to visit his advisor. Yeah, I let him talk me into it. My knight made me see that I can't just exist forever. I guess he's right. I can't spend my life just living. Oh, don't get me wrong, Le-Le is going to live for now. I'm going to hang with my crew and drink and party. But when the time comes, I'll figure out what I want to do with my future. Nessa says I should open up a restaurant. We'll see. But when I decide, I will decide on my own. I don't need anyone telling me how to live my life. Now that I know the possibilities and choices are endless.

Printed in the United States
18876LVS00001B/388-405